Crown Imperial:
Majesty and Power

Majesty and power had been
barriers separating His Royal
Highness Alexander and
Eve Hamilton, a beautiful
commoner. Seven years of
silence came between them,
until an assassination threat
gave theatrical producer Eve
a new role to play—and this
time, she'd be giving the
performance of her life!

NORA ROBERTS
LANGUAGE OF LOVE

**Love has a language all its own, and for
centuries, flowers have symbolized
love's finest expression.
Discover the language of flowers
—and love—
in this romantic collection of 48 favorite
books by bestselling author Nora Roberts.**

1. Lily of the Valley
   IRISH THOROUGHBRED
2. Hollyhock THE LAW IS A LADY
3. Cabbage Rose IRISH ROSE
4. Wallflower STORM WARNING
5. Foxglove FIRST IMPRESSIONS
6. Yellow Jasmine REFLECTIONS
7. Marigold NIGHT MOVES
8. Narcissus DANCE OF DREAMS
9. China Aster OPPOSITES ATTRACT
10. Amaryllis ISLAND OF FLOWERS
11. Great Yellow Daffodil
    SEARCH FOR LOVE
12. Hyacinth PLAYING THE ODDS
13. Gloxinia TEMPTING FATE
14. Forget-me-not FROM THIS DAY
15. Petunia ALL THE POSSIBILITIES
16. Tuberose HEART'S VICTORY
17. Red Poppy ONE MAN'S ART
18. Gladiola RULES OF THE GAME
19. White Periwinkle
    FOR NOW, FOREVER
20. Pansy HER MOTHER'S KEEPER
21. Orchid PARTNERS
22. Stock SULLIVAN'S WOMAN
23. Dahlia SUMMER DESSERTS
24. Iris THIS MAGIC MOMENT
25. Pink LESSONS LEARNED
26. Lavender THE RIGHT PATH
27. Love in a Mist
    THE ART OF DECEPTION
28. Azalea UNTAMED
29. Red Carnation DUAL IMAGE
30. Bluebell SECOND NATURE
31. Red and White Roses
    ONE SUMMER
32. Wisteria GABRIEL'S ANGEL
33. Trumpet Flower
    THE NAME OF THE GAME
34. Purple Columbine
    A WILL AND A WAY
35. Honeysuckle AFFAIRE ROYALE
36. Spring Crocus
    LESS OF A STRANGER
37. Crown Imperial
    COMMAND PERFORMANCE
38. White Camellia BLITHE IMAGES
39. Cyclamen THE PLAYBOY PRINCE
40. Purple Lilac TREASURES LOST,
    TREASURES FOUND
41. White Daisy RISKY BUSINESS
42. Red Tulip LOVING JACK
43. Apple Blossom TEMPTATION
44. Dogwood BEST LAID PLANS
45. Clematis MIND OVER MATTER
46. Garden Anemone THE WELCOMING
47. Snapdragon BOUNDARY LINES
48. Morning Glory LOCAL HERO

NORA ROBERTS

LANGUAGE OF LOVE

COMMAND
PERFORMANCE

Silhouette Books®

To Walter Mittermeyer, a true prince,
and his lady, Helen

SILHOUETTE BOOKS
300 East 42nd St., New York, N.Y. 10017

COMMAND PERFORMANCE © 1987 by Nora Roberts.
First published as a Silhouette Intimate Moments.

Language of Love edition published December 1991.

ISBN: 0-373-51037-3

Chapter One

She'd been to the palace before. The first time, nearly seven years earlier, she'd thought it was a fairy tale sprung into three dimensions. She was older now, though she wasn't sure about wiser. Cordina was a country. The palace was a building, a beautiful one. Fairy tales were for the very young, the very naive or the very fortunate.

Despite the fact that she knew the palace that housed the royal family of Cordina was stone and mortar rather than wishes and dreams, she had to admire it. It glistened white, almost pristine, atop a jagged jut of land that overlooked both sea and town. Almost pristine, yes, but not detached—and not altogether placid.

Towers speared to the sky, piercing the blue with white. Turrets and buttresses attested to its age-old defensive function. The moat had been filled in, but one could imagine it. In its place were high-tech security systems and surveillance. Windows, some clear, some tinted, gleamed. Like any palace, there had been triumph and tragedy there, intrigue and glamour. It still stunned her that she'd had some part in it.

On her first visit she had walked on a terrace with a prince and, as fate had dictated, had had some part in saving his life. Fate, Eve decided as her limo passed through the high iron gates and beyond the red uniformed guards, was always sticking its fingers into ordinary lives.

Circumstances had led her to the tiny principality of Cordina all those years before, accompanying her sister, Chris, an old friend and schoolmate of the Princess Gabriella. If the circumstances had been different, Prince

Bennett might have been with another woman on the terrace that night. She might never have met him or become a part of the closing chapters of the political intrigue that had haunted his sister and the rest of the royal family.

She might never have developed a fondness for the lovely palace in the storybook country. She might never have found herself being drawn back to it time and again. Yet this time she hadn't been drawn back exactly. She'd been called back. Command performance. She wrinkled her nose at the thought. Wasn't it too bad the command had to come from the one member of the royal family who annoyed her.

Prince Alexander, eldest son of the reigning monarch and heir to the throne. She watched trees heavy with pink blossoms bend in the breeze as the car cruised by. His Royal Highness Alexander Robert Armand de Cordina. She couldn't say where she'd learned his full name or why she remembered it. To Eve, it was simply as rigid and humorless a title as the man it pertained to.

A pity he wasn't more like his brother. Just thinking of Bennett made her smile and look forward to the visit. Bennett was charming and approachable. He didn't wear that invisible, but somehow tangible crown every minute of the day. Alexander was like his father—duty, country, family. That didn't leave much time for relaxation.

Well, she wasn't here to relax, either. She was here to talk to Alexander, and to talk business. Times had changed, and she wasn't a young, impressionable girl who could be awed by royalty or hurt by unspoken disapproval. No, Alexander was too well-bred ever to speak his disapproval, but no one Eve had ever known could convey it more clearly. If she hadn't wanted to spend a few days in Cordina again, she would have insisted that he come to Houston. Eve preferred discussing business on her own turf and on her own terms.

With a smile she stepped from the limo. Since she'd given up the first, she'd just have to make sure she won the second. Dueling with Alexander, and winning, would certainly be a pleasure.

The palace doors opened just as she started up the wide stone steps. Eve stopped. Her dark blue eyes took on a wicked light as she dipped into a deep curtsy. "Your Highness."

"Eve." With a quick, pleasant laugh Bennett bounded down the steps to her.

He'd been with the horses again, she thought as his arms went around her. Their scent clung to him, earthy and real. When she'd met him seven years before, he'd been a beautiful young man with an eye for the ladies and a good time. Drawing back to look at him, she saw he was older certainly, but little else had changed.

"It's so good to see you." He kissed her hard, but the passion was friendship and nothing more. "Too long between visits, Eve. It's been two years since you've been in Cordina."

"I'm a working woman, Bennett." She slid her hands down to clasp his. "How are you? If looks mean anything, you're marvelous. And if the scandal sheets mean anything, you're very busy."

"All true." He grinned and his clean-lined, almost poetic face became irresistible. "Come inside, I'll fix you a drink. No one's told me how long you're staying."

"That's because I'm not sure myself. It depends."

Her arm hooked through his, she entered the palace. It was cool, white and wide. Stairs swept up the side of the main hall, curling up and beyond the lofty ceiling. She'd always felt steady here, secure with the flavor of antiquity, continuity. Tapestries stretched over the walls, swords crossed with blades gleaming. A Louis XIV table held a bowl of distressed silver overflowing with jasmine.

"How was your flight?"

"Mmmm. Long." They turned off the main hall into a parlor where the drapes were open wide and the sun spilled in. The rays had long since beaten into the upholstery and faded it comfortably. There were roses here, rising out of porcelain and crystal. Eve dropped onto a sofa and drew in the scent. "Let's say I'm glad to be on the ground, glad to be here. Tell me how everyone is, Ben. Your sister?"

"Brie's wonderful. She'd planned to meet you at the airport, but her youngest has the sniffles." He chose a bottle of dry vermouth and poured it over ice. One of his greatest charms was never forgetting a woman's preferences. "It's still hard, after all these years, to picture my sister as a mother—especially a mother of four."

"I've a letter from Chris and orders to hand-deliver it. She also wants a full report on her goddaughter."

"Let's see which one is that? Ah, Camilla. I can tell you firsthand she's a scamp. Drives her brothers mad."

"That's what sisters are for." Smiling, she accepted the drink. "And Reeve?"

"He's fine, though there's no doubt he'd be more comfortable if they were settled year-round in America on that farm of his. They've done some pretty incredible things with the little farm here, but Brie's still official hostess in Cordina. Reeve would like nothing better than for Alex to marry and shift those duties onto his wife."

"Or you." She sipped, watching him over the rim. "If you took the plunge, some of Brie's responsibilities would shift."

"I love her, but not that much." He sprawled on the sofa, kicking his long, booted legs out.

"No truth to the rumors about Lady Alice Winthrop, then? Or was it the Honorable Jessica Mansfield most recently?"

"Lovely girls," he said easily. "I notice you're tactful enough not to mention the Countess Milano."

"She's ten years older than you." Her tone took on that of a lecturing aunt, but she smiled. "And I'm always tactful."

"So what about you, Eve?" When things came that close to the bone, Bennett was the master of evasion. "How does someone who looks like you manage to keep men at arm's length?''

"Karate. Black belt, seventh degree."

"Yes, I'd forgotten about that."

"You shouldn't have. I decked you twice."

"Oh, no. It was only once." He tossed his arm over the back of the sofa and looked as he was, arrogant, comfortable and sure of himself. "And I let you."

"It was twice." She sipped again. "And you were furious."

"Luck," he said firmly. "Added to the fact that as a gentleman, I couldn't hurt a woman."

"Bull."

"My dear, a hundred years ago you might have lost your head, lovely as it is."

"Your Highness," she said, and smiled with him, "you stop being a gentleman the moment there's competition. If you could have thrown me first, you would have."

It was true enough. "Care to try it again?"

A dare was something she could never, would never be able to ignore. Eve took a last sip of vermouth and rose. "At your service."

Bennett stood and with one foot shoved the table away from the couch. After tossing back his untidy hair with one hand, he narrowed his eyes. "Now as I recall, I was to come up from behind and grab...just here." One tightly muscled arm hooked around her midriff. "Then I—"

The rest was cut off as she knocked his foot out from under him and sent him flat on his back. "Yes." She brushed her palms together as she looked down at him. "That's precisely as I remember it."

"I wasn't ready." He propped himself on an elbow.

"All's fair, Your Highness." With a laugh she knelt beside him. "Did I hurt you?"

"Only my pride," he muttered, and gave her hair a tug.

When Alexander walked in, he saw his brother sprawled on the Turkish carpet, his hand intimately twined in Eve's dark fall of hair. Their faces were close, smiling, their bodies just brushing. His jaw set, then tightened.

"I apologize for interrupting."

At his voice Bennett looked languidly over his shoulder, and Eve's shoulders snapped straight. He looked precisely as she remembered, dark, thick hair curling down his neck and over his ears. He wasn't smiling, though he rarely did that she'd seen, so that his face was rigidly handsome. Royalty suited him. Even as she resented it, she had to acknowledge it. He might have been one of the portraits she remembered from the palace gallery—high cheekbones well defined, the skin tanned and smooth over them. His eyes were dark, almost as dark as his hair, and as disapproving as his full, sculpted mouth, which was drawn now in a tight line. As always, he was militarily straight and impeccably dressed.

She felt mussed and travel stained and foolish.

"Eve's been giving me another lesson in the martial arts." Bennett rose, then taking Eve's hand, pulled her up beside him. "I've come out second best. Again."

"So I see." His bow was formal and just this side of polite. "Miss Hamilton."

She curtsied, but there was no gleam of humor in her eyes this time. "Your Highness."

"I apologize for not being able to meet you at the airport. I trust your flight was pleasant."

"Delightful."

"Perhaps you'd like to freshen up before we discuss the reason I sent for you."

That brought her chin up. He'd hoped it would. Deliberately she reached down and picked up the small envelope bag she'd left on the sofa. "I'd prefer to get our business over with."

"As you wish. We'll go up to my office. Bennett, aren't you speaking at the Equestrian Society today?"

"Not for a couple of hours." He turned and gave Eve a friendly kiss on the nose, sending her a wink only she could see and appreciate. "I'll see you at dinner. Wear something dazzling, will you?"

"Naturally." But her smiled faded as she turned back to Alexander. "Your Highness?"

Inclining his head, he gestured her from the room.

They climbed the staircase in silence. He was angry. Eve was perceptive enough to understand that without understanding the reason for it. Though two years had passed since they'd been face to face, he was as stiffly disapproving of her as he'd always been. Because she was an American? she wondered. No, Reeve MacGee was an American and he had married Alexander's sister. Because she was in the theater?

Eve's lips curled a bit at the thought. It would be just like him. Cordina boasted one of the best theater complexes in the world in the Fine Arts Center, but Alexander could easily be disdainful of people in the theater. Tossing her head back, she entered his office just ahead of him.

"Coffee?"

"No, thank you."

"Please, sit."

She did, but kept her back ramrod straight. His office reflected him, with its elegantly conservative style. There were no frills, no flounces. The only scents were coffee and leather. The furniture was old and glossy, the rug thick and faded with age. Tall glass doors led to a balcony, but they were closed now, as if he had no desire for the sound of the sea or the fragrance of the garden.

The signs of wealth didn't intimidate her. She'd come from wealth and had since earned her own. It was the formality that had her sitting rigidly and waiting for the attack.

"Your sister is well?" Alexander took out a cigarette, then lifted a brow.

Eve nodded and waited as he struck a match. "She's very well. She plans to spend some time with Gabriella's family when they return to America. Bennett told me one of the children is ill."

"Dorian. A head cold." For the first time his features softened. Of all his sister's children, it was the youngest who held the strongest grip on his heart. "He isn't easily kept in bed."

"I'd like to see the children before I leave. I haven't seen any of them since Dorian was christened."

"Two years ago." He remembered, perhaps too well. "I'm sure we can arrange for you to visit the farm." When her lips curved, he drew back. He was no longer indulgent uncle or casual friend, but prince. "My father's away. He sends you his best if he hasn't returned before you leave."

"I read he was in Paris."

"Yes." He closed the door on state business without ever having opened it. "I appreciate your coming here, as it wasn't possible for me to travel at this time. My secretary outlined my proposal?"

"Yes, he did." Business, Eve reminded herself. The amenities, such as they were, were over. "You'd like me to bring my troupe to Cordina for a month's run of performances at the Fine Arts Center. The performances would be for the benefit of The Aid to Handicapped Children."

"That's correct."

"Forgive me, Your Highness, but I was under the impression that Princess Gabriella was in charge of this particular charity."

"She is. I am president of the Fine Arts Center. On this we work together." It was as much explanation as he would give. "Gabriella saw your troupe perform in America and was impressed. She felt that since Cordina has such a strong bond with the United States, using American performers in our country would help bring in desperately needed funds for the AHC."

"So this is her idea."

"One, after long discussions and consideration, I've decided to agree with."

"I see." One rounded nail began to tap on the arm of her chair. "I take that to mean you had reservations."

"I've never seen your troupe perform." He leaned back slightly and blew out a stream of smoke. "We've had American entertainers at the center before, of course, but never for this length of time or as a prelude to the AHC ball."

"Maybe you'd like us to audition."

His lips relaxed slightly, interestingly, into a smile. "It had crossed my mind."

"I think not." She rose, and noted with pleasure that manners forced him to stand, as well. "The Hamilton troupe has, in less than five years, earned both critical and popular approval. We have a reputation for excellence that requires no auditions in your country or any. If I decide to bring my company here, it will be because I respect the AHC and Gabriella."

He watched her as she spoke. She'd changed in seven years from a wide-eyed young girl into a confident woman. Yet somehow, astonishingly, she was even more beautiful. Her skin was flawless, pale, with hints of rose at the crest of her cheekbones. Her face was diamond shaped and just as stunning as the gem, with a full rich mouth and huge poetically blue eyes. Framing it was a mane of luxuriant black hair, a bit mussed now as it tumbled to her shoulders and beyond.

Temper kept her standing straight, but her body was delicate, or so it seemed. He'd wondered, he'd wondered too often, what it would feel like against his.

Even in anger her voice carried the slow, Texas drawl he'd learned to recognize. It breezed soft over his skin until the muscles in his stomach contracted. Carefully, relying on the control he'd fought to develop all his life, Alexander crushed out his cigarette.

"If you've finished, Miss Hamilton?"

"Eve, for Lord's sake. We've known each other for years." Out of patience she stalked over to the balcony doors and shoved them open. Facing the outside, she didn't notice Alexander's brows raise at her breech of protocol, or the slow smile.

"Eve," he said, then let her name hang on the air a moment. "I think we've misunderstood each other. I'm not criticizing your company. That would be difficult, because, as I said, I've never seen them perform."

"At this rate you never will."

"Then I'd have to deal with Brie's temper. I prefer not to. Sit down." When she merely turned and looked at him, he checked his impulse to command and gestured to her chair. "Please."

She obeyed, but left the doors open. The sea could just be heard. The scent of rose, vanilla and spice wafted up from the gardens. "I'm sitting," she said, and crossed her legs.

He disapproved of her curt, one-to-one manner. He admired her independence. At the moment Alexander wasn't sure how the two could be mixed. He was sure that she stirred, as she always did, something more than polite emotions in him. Slowly he took his seat again and faced her.

"As a member of the royal family and as president of the Fine Arts Center, I must be very discreet and very circumspect in whom I choose to perform. In this case I'm trusting Gabriella's judgment and asking you if we can come to an arrangement."

"Perhaps." Eve was a businesswoman first and last. Personal feelings had never swayed her decisions, and they wouldn't now. "I'll have to see the theater again, check out the facilities. I'll have to be assured contractually that I and my company have artistic freedom—and adequate lodging during the run. Because the performances would be for a charity, I'm willing to negotiate our fee and expenses. Artistically, however, there is no negotiation."

"I'll see to it that you have a tour of the center. The center's lawyers and yours can deal with the contract. Artistically..." He linked his fingers on the desk. "Because you are the artist, I'll respect your judgment, but I'm not willing to toss myself blindly into your hands. The idea is for your company to perform four plays, one week each. The material will have to be approved by the center."

"By you."

It was a negligent, imperial shrug. "As you like."

She didn't like, and didn't bother to pretend otherwise. "What are your qualifications?"

"I beg your pardon?"

"What do you know about the theater? You're a politician." She said it with a faint, very faint, sneer of contempt. "Why should I bring my company here, thousands of miles from home, for a fraction of what we normally earn so that you can pick and choose the material we perform?"

His temper had never been easily harnessed. Through years of dedication and determination he'd learned how to channel it. He did so now without taking his eyes from hers. "Because performing at the Fine Arts Center in Cordina at the request of the royal family would be a career advantage you would be foolish to ignore." He leaned forward. "I don't believe you're a foolish woman, Eve."

"No, I'm not." She rose again, but slowly, then waited until he stood on the other side of his desk. "I'll see the theater first, and I'll think about it before I ask the members of my troupe."

"You run the company, don't you?"

She tilted her head and a lock of hair fell over one eye. With her fingertips she drew it back. "You forget, America's a democracy, Your Highness. I don't hand down decrees to my people. If I find the facilities adequate and my troupe agrees, we'll talk contracts. Now if you'll excuse me, I'd like to unpack and change before dinner."

"I'll have someone show you to your rooms."

"I know where they are." She stopped at the door, turned and dropped an arrogant curtsy. "Your Highness."

"Eve." He watched her chin jut out. One day, he thought, someone was going to take her up on it. "Welcome to Cordina."

* * *

She wasn't a rude person. Eve assured herself of it as she chose a dress for dinner. In fact, she was considered amiable by just about everyone. True, she could get hard-nosed in business dealings, but she'd always considered that in the blood. She wasn't rude. Except with Alexander.

He asked for it, she told herself as she zipped into a snug, strapless dress in vivid blue silk. He was so aloof and condescending. She didn't have to tolerate that, heir to the throne or not. They were hardly playing prince and the pauper here. Her pedigree might not be royal, but it was unimpeachable.

She'd gone to the best schools. Maybe she'd hated them, but she'd gone. She'd entertained and been entertained by the rich, powerful and influential all her life. And she'd made something of herself. Not through her family, but through her own skills.

True, she'd discovered early on that her ambition to be an actress was never going to bear very ripe fruit, but her love of the theater hadn't ebbed. Added to that had been her innate business and organizational skills. The Hamilton Company of Players had been born and had flourished. She didn't appreciate Alexander the Great coming along and acting as though he were doing her a favor letting her troupe perform in his center.

They'd performed at Lincoln Center, the Kennedy Center, the Mark Taper Forum, and to solid reviews.

She'd worked hard to find the best, to develop talent, to stretch her own boundaries, and he came along and nodded graciously. Scowling, she hooked a thick gold collar around her neck. The Hamilton Company of Players didn't need his approval, gracious or otherwise.

She didn't need his approval or his damn royal seal. And she would be unbearably stupid to refuse to perform in Cordina.

Eve picked up a brush and dragged it through her hair. It was then that she noticed she had only one earring on. He was making her crazy, she decided, and found the teardrop sapphire on her dresser.

Why wasn't Ben president of the center? Why wasn't Brie still handling it? With either she could have been easy and relaxed. The job, if she chose to do it, could be done professionally, but without the added headache. What was it about Alexander that set her teeth on edge?

Eve fastened the second earring in place and frowned at her reflection. She could still remember the first time she'd seen him. She'd been twenty, and though he'd been only a few years older, he'd seemed so adult, so dashing. Bennett had led her out for the first dance at the ball, but it had been Alexander she'd watched. She'd been fanciful then, Eve admitted, imagining him as just the sort of prince who rescued damsels in distress and killed dragons. He'd had a sword at his side, for decoration only, but she had seen in her mind how he would wield it.

The crush had come quickly and, thank God, had been gone just as fast. She might have been fanciful, but as Alexander himself had said, she wasn't foolish. No woman pinned her dreams on the unyielding and disapproving. It had been easy to turn her attention to Bennett.

A pity they hadn't fallen in love, she thought now. Princess Eve. Laughing at herself, she dropped the brush. No, that just didn't fit. Luckily for everyone, she and Bennett had become friends before they had become anything else.

And she had the troupe. It was more than an ambition—it was a purpose. She'd watched friends marry and divorce and marry again, or simply drift from one affair to the next. Too often the reason was simple boredom. She'd never had to worry about that. Running the company would take up twenty-four hours a day if she allowed it. At times it came close, whether she wanted it to or not. If she was attracted to a man, her business and her own caution kept things from getting too serious. So she hadn't made a mistake. Yet. She didn't intend to.

Eve picked up her perfume and sprayed it over her bare shoulders before she left the room.

With luck Bennett would be back and lounging in the parlor. Dinner wouldn't be dull with him around, nor would it be strained for very long. He added spark and enjoyment simply by being. She wasn't in love with him, but she loved him for that.

As she walked downstairs she trailed her fingers along the smooth banister. So many fingers had trailed there before. When she was inside the palace, she thought of it only as a place, a sturdy, eternal place. If she understood little about Alexander, she understood his pride.

But when she stepped into the parlor and found him there alone, she tensed. Stopping in the doorway, she scanned the room for Bennett.

Good God, she was beautiful. When Alexander turned, it hit him like a blow. It had nothing to do with the silk, with the jewels. She could have dressed in burlap and still stunned the senses. Dark, sultry, just edging over to hot, there was something primitive, something uncomfortably natural about her sexuality that made a man ache just looking. It had been part of her since she had been hardly more than a child. Alexander decided she'd been born with it and cursed her for it.

His body tightened, his face settled into cool lines, as he saw her gaze sweep the room. He knew she was looking for, hoping for, Bennett.

"My brother's been detained." He stood with his back to a scrubbed hearth. The dark dinner jacket both suited and restrained him. "We dine alone this evening."

Eve stood where she was, as though stepping forward were a commitment she was far from ready to make. "There's no need to trouble for me, Your Highness. I can easily have dinner in my room if you'd like to make other plans."

"You're my guest. My plans are to dine with you." He turned away to pour drinks. "Come in, Eve. I promise you, I won't wrestle with you on the floor."

"I'm sure you won't," she said just as politely. Crossing to him, she held her hand out for the drink. "And we weren't wrestling. I threw him."

Deliberately he swept his gaze down. She was willow slender and barely higher than his shoulder. He wouldn't believe she'd thrown his tall, athletic brother physically. But emotionally was another matter. "Admirable. Then I'll promise I won't give you the opportunity to throw me. Your rooms are agreeable?"

"Perfect, as always. As I recall, you rarely have free evenings at home. No state dinners or official functions tonight?"

He glanced at her again. The lights were dim, so that they gave her skin the sheen of satin. Perhaps it would feel the same. "We could consider dining with you an official function, if you like."

"Perhaps I do." She watched him over the rim as she sipped. "So, Your Highness, do we make polite conversation or discuss world politics?"

"Politics at dinner make for an uneasy appetite. Especially when they're at odds."

"That's true. We never have agreed on many things. Polite conversation, then." She'd been schooled in it, as he had. Strolling to the bowl of roses, she stroked the petals. "I read that you were in Switzerland a few weeks during the winter. How was the skiing?"

"Excellent." He didn't add his real reason for being there, or mention the hours of meetings and discussions. He tried not to look at her long, slender fingers against the deep red roses. "Do you ski?"

"I get to Colorado now and again." The movement of her shoulders was negligent and noncommittal. How could she expect him to understand that she didn't have the time for idle games and casual trips? "I haven't been to Switzerland since I got out of school there. Being from Houston, I prefer summer sports."

"Such as?"

"Swimming."

"Then I should tell you the pool is at your disposal during your stay."

"Thank you." Silence. Eve felt her body tensing as it dragged on. "We seem to be out of polite conversation, and we haven't even had dinner."

"Then perhaps we should." He offered his arm, and though she hesitated, Eve slipped hers through it. "The cook recalled that you were particularly fond of his *poisson bonne femme*."

"Really? How nice." She unbent enough to smile up at him. "As I recall, I was more particularly fond of his *pôts de crème au chocolat*. I drove my father's cook mad until she could come up with a reasonable facsimile."

"Then you should be pleased with tonight's dessert."

"I'll be fat," she corrected, then stopped at the entrance to the dining room. "I've always admired this room," Eve murmured. "It's so ageless, so permanent." She studied it again, the two glistening chandeliers that spilled light onto a massive table and lovingly polished floors. The size didn't intimidate her, though more than a hundred could fit at the table.

As a rule, she might prefer the cozy, the more intimate, but the room had such power. Because she had grown up with it, power was something she expected as well as respected. But it was more the very age of the room that fascinated her. If she were very still, very quiet, she thought she could almost hear the conversations that had gone on there through the centuries.

"The first time I had dinner here, I was shaking like a leaf."

"Were you?" Interested, he didn't usher her in, but stayed at the entrance beside her. "I remember you being remarkably composed."

"Oh, I've always been good at false fronts, but inside I was terrified. Here I was, fresh out of school and having dinner in a palace."

"And this time?"

She wasn't sure why it was necessary, but she slipped her arm from his. "I've been out of school quite a while."

Two places were set at the table with candelabras and fresh flowers. Eve took her place at the side and left the head for Alexander. As they sat, a servant poured wine.

"It seems odd," she said after a moment. "Whenever I've been here before, the palace has been full of people."

"Gabriella and Reeve rarely stay here now that they're settled at the farm. Or farms," he corrected. "They split their time between their countries."

"Are they happy?"

His brow rose as he picked up his glass. "Happy?"

"Yes, you know, happy. It comes somewhere down the list after duty and obligation."

He waited silently as plates of chilled lobster were served. She had been too close to the mark with her talk of lists. He could never put his happiness before his duty, his feelings before his obligations. "My sister doesn't complain. She loves her husband, her children and her country."

"That's not the same thing."

"The family have done their best to lessen some of her duties."

"It's wonderful, isn't it, that after that terrible time she went through, she has everything." She saw his knuckles whiten on his fork, and reached automatically for his hand. "I'm sorry. Even after all this time it must be difficult to think of."

He said nothing a moment, just looked down at her hand, white, slender, covering his. It soothed. He'd never expected that. If it had been possible for him, he would have turned his over to grip hers. "It will always be difficult to think of, and impossible to forget that you were a part of saving both my sister and my brother."

"I only ran for help."

"You kept your head. If you hadn't we would have lost both of them."

"I'll never forget it, either." Realizing her hand was still on his, Eve drew it away and made a business out of picking up her wine. "I can still see that woman's face."

"Deboque's lover."

He said it with such restrained violence, she shuddered. "Yes. The way she looked when she was holding that gun on Brie. That's when I realized palaces weren't just fairy tales. I'm sure you're all glad she and Loubet and Deboque are in prison."

"And will remain there. But Deboque has pulled strings from behind bars before."

"Has there been more? Bennett and I have spoken of it, but—"

"Bennett needs lessons in discretion."

She flared, swallowing a retort as one course was cleared and another served. "He didn't reveal any state secrets. We were simply remembering once—just as you and I are now— that Deboque had been in prison but had arranged for Brie's kidnapping through her secretary and your father's minister of state. He said he'd be uneasy as long as Deboque was alive. I told him it was nonsense, but maybe I was wrong."

"To be a public figure is to be uneasy." It was simpler to accept that than to remember his own feeling of helplessness, of watching his sister struggle through her trauma and pain. "The Bissets have ruled Cordina for generations. As long as we do, we make enemies. All of them are not, cannot be, in prison."

There was more. She sensed it but knew better than to try to make Alexander open up to her. If she wanted to know, when she wanted to know, she would go to Bennett. "It sounds like commoners have the advantage, Your Highness."

"Yes." With a smile she didn't understand, he picked up his fork.

* * *

They dined companionably enough, more companionably than Eve would have imagined. He didn't relax. She wondered about that as they eased through courses toward dessert and coffee. He was pleasant, polite—and on edge. She wanted to help, to ease away the tension so obvious in the set of his shoulders. But he wasn't a man to accept help from an outsider.

He would rule one day, and had been born to do it. Cordina was a small, storybook country, but like a storybook, it had its share of intrigue and unrest. What he'd been destined to do didn't sit on him lightly. Her background and upbringing made it difficult to comprehend, so that often, perhaps too often, she saw only the unbending outer layer.

At least they hadn't argued, Eve thought as she toyed with dessert. Actually, one didn't argue with Alexander; one just fumed and batted against a stone wall.

"That was lovely. Your cook only improves with time."

"He'll be pleased to hear it." He wanted her to stay, just to sit and talk about anything that wasn't important. For the last hour he'd nearly forgotten the pressure he was under. It wasn't like him, but the thought of going up to his rooms, to his work, was unappealing. "If you're not tired—"

"You didn't eat it all, did you?" Bennett bounded in and pulled up the chair beside Eve. "Done?" Without waiting, he took the rest of her dessert. "The food they pushed on me doesn't bear thinking about. I could picture the two of you here while I was eating rubber chicken."

"You don't look deprived," Eve noted, and smiled at him. "The main course was exquisite."

"You always had a nasty streak. Look, after I've finished this, let's go outside. I need the garden and a beautiful woman after hours at that stuffy meeting."

"If you two will excuse me, then." Alexander rose. "I'll leave you alone."

"Take a walk with us, Alex," Bennett invited. "After I finish the rest of your mousse."

"Not tonight. I've work."

"Always does," Bennett murmured. He reached for Alexander's dessert as Eve turned and watched the prince leave. She couldn't have said why, but she had an urge to follow him. Shaking the feeling off, she turned back to laugh at Bennett.

Chapter Two

"When Alexander promised me a tour guide, I didn't expect it to be you."

Her Serene Highness Gabriella de Cordina laughed as she pushed open the stage door. "The center's been a family affair from the beginning. Actually, I think Alex would have liked to take you through himself if his schedule hadn't been so full."

Eve let that pass, thinking Alexander would prefer mounds of paperwork and hours of stuffy meetings to an hour with her. "I hate to repeat myself, Brie, but you look wonderful."

"Repeat yourself," Gabriella told her. "When you've had four children you need all the moral support you can get." Her dark red hair was pinned up in a sleek, simple knot and her white suit was carefully tailored. She was every inch a princess. Still, Eve thought she looked too young and too fragile to have borne four children. "And you," she continued, stopping a moment to study the sister of her closest friend. "I remember the first time I saw you. I thought, what a stunning child. Now you're a stunning woman. Chris has nearly stopped worrying about you."

"I used to hate that." She could smile now, remembering the tug of war with her sister during her long, rebellious youth. "Now that I'm older, I find myself hoping she never stops worrying completely. It's so comforting. Isn't it strange that family comes to mean more to you as an adult?"

"I don't know what I'd do without mine. Those few months that I couldn't remember them, couldn't remember anything..." Gabriella trailed off with a shake of her head. "It's taught me to take nothing for granted. Well." She drew a deep breath and looked around. "What would you like to see first?"

"Let's take the backstage area—dressing rooms, fly. I'll take a look at the light board. If things don't work back here, it doesn't matter how good you are out front."

"You know what you're doing, don't you?"

"Let's hope so."

They spent over an hour backstage. Eve climbed stairs, squeezed into storerooms, examined equipment. It was, as she'd hoped, top rate. The Fine Arts Center was a family affair, built in the name of Gabriella's mother. The Bissets had poured their love for her into making it one of the best theater complexes in the world.

Eve felt the excitement growing. To play here would top anything she or the company had ever done. Already her mind was leaping forward. She would produce four typically American plays for an international audience. The company publicist would have a field day with promotion. Tennessee Williams, Neil Simon, Arthur Miller. She had such a wealth of talent to choose from. And she'd want her own technicians on the lights, on the ropes, on the props.

"I can see the wheels turning," Gabriella murmured.

"I've never been subtle." Eve walked out, stood stage center and let herself feel.

It was incredible, the sensations, the vibrations that hung in the air of an empty theater. This one had been designed for the actor. She could almost smell the greasepaint and the sweat. The seats rolled forward, slashed through by three wide aisles that were carpeted in royal blue. The houselights were enormous chandeliers and the ceilings were frescoed. Box seats tilted out of the walls on either side and straight back was a balcony. Even from the distance she could see the railings were hand carved and gleaming. More important, every seat in the house would have an unobstructed view of the stage.

"'Tonight, it ends here, miserably. Whatever we've done, whatever we've attempted to do, no longer matters. When tomorrow comes, it begins again, and we—we will never have existed.'"

Her voice flowed out, back to the corners, up to the last row of the balcony, then echoed back. Satisfied, Eve smiled.

"Wonderful." She turned back to Brie. "Whoever your architect was, he deserves a medal."

"I'll suggest it to my father. Eve, what was that from? I don't recognize it."

"You wouldn't. Struggling playwright." She passed it off quickly, not wanting to say the struggling playwright was herself. "Brie, the theater's wonderful. Another time I'd love to do something on that smaller stage downstairs. Something intimate. But for our purposes, this is perfect."

"Oh, I was hoping you'd say that." Gabriella's heels clicked as she crossed the stage to Eve. "Ever since Alex and I kicked the idea around, I've been waiting for that. Eve, we're going to do something important, for your company, for our countries, for the children."

"I'm only going to put on some plays," Eve corrected, squeezing Gabriella's hand. "I'll leave the higher causes to you and Alex. But if we can get the details ironed out, the contracts, and the legalities of it, you're going to see four terrific productions."

"I'm counting on it."

She took one last glance around the stage. She would never perform here, but her company would. One day, maybe one day, one of her own plays would be acted here. She nearly laughed at herself for the fantasy. "Then I'd better get back home and start working."

"Oh, no, we're not letting you go so quickly. I've already planned a family dinner at the farm. Tomorrow night. Now..." She hooked her arm through Eve's. "I want you to go back and be lazy for the rest of the day. Once we put you to work, you won't have another opportunity."

"Is that a royal command?"

"Absolutely."

"Then I'll just have to suffer through it."

It wasn't so hard. Eve discovered that lounging by the pool while a balmy Mediterranean breeze ruffled the palm fronds overhead wasn't such a tough job. In her youth she'd done a lot of lounging. Vegetating, Eve corrected. It amazed her that she had been content to do nothing for such long periods of time. Not that there was anything wrong with doing nothing, she added as she adjusted her chaise one more notch back. It was just a pity to make a career out of it.

She nearly had. Affluence, privilege. It had made it so easy to sit and let others do. She might have continued in just that vein if she hadn't discovered the theater. It had given her something to start at the bottom in, something to work toward. Something Daddy, bless him, couldn't wrangle for her. She could either act or she couldn't. Eve had discovered she could. But it hadn't been stage center where she'd found her niche.

Theater had opened up worlds for her, worlds inside herself. She was competent; she was shrewd; she was blessed with organizational talents she'd never used during her education. Conceiving her own company, bringing it to life, had sharpened all those skills. It had also taught her how to take risks, work hard, and mostly, how to be dependable. There were people relying on her for their art and for their living. The responsibility had turned a spoiled young girl into a dedicated woman.

Now she was being given the opportunity to reap rewards even she hadn't dreamed of. International recognition for her company. All she had to do was select the right material, produce four plays, handle four sets of wardrobe, four sets of props, four sets of scenery. In the meantime she had to deal with lawyers, directors, transportation, seventy-odd actors and technicians. And a prince.

Eve pushed her sunglasses farther up on her nose and sighed. What was life without a few challenges?

He shouldn't have come out. One look at his watch told Alexander he had an appointment in twenty minutes. He had no business going out to the pool when he should have been in his office, preparing for the meeting with the minister of state. He should have known better than to ask, however casually, if Miss Hamilton had returned from the center. He should have known better than to think he could have gone up to his office and concentrated once he knew she was out at the pool.

She looked as though she were sleeping. The brief red bikini stretched low over her hips, rose high at the thighs. She'd untied the straps to the top so that it stayed in place only because of her prone position. He couldn't see her eyes behind the sunglasses, but she made no movement at all when he approached.

He looked his fill. Her skin was glistening with the oil she'd applied to every exposed area. Its scent rose exotically to compete with the flowers. Her hair curled damp and dark around her face, showing him she hadn't sat idly, but had used the pool. Stepping closer, he saw her eyes flutter open beneath the amber-tinted lenses.

"You should take more care. You're not accustomed to our Mediterranean sun."

She lay almost flat on her back, staring up at him. He blocked the sun now, so that it glowed like a nimbus around his head. She blinked, trying to clear her vision and her brain. Damsels in distress and dragons. She thought of them again, though he looked more like a god than a prince.

"I thought you were out." She propped herself up on her elbow before she remembered her bikini. As it slipped, she grabbed for it with one hand and swore. He simply stood there while she struggled with the ties and what was left of her modesty.

"I was out. You're skin's very white, Eve. You'll burn quickly."

It occurred to her that protocol demanded she rise and curtsy. Protocol aside, a curtsy in a bikini wasn't practical. She stayed as she was. "I've slathered on a pint of sunscreen, and I wasn't intending to stay out much longer. Besides, living in Houston toughens the skin."

"It hasn't appeared to." Minister of state or not, Alexander pulled a chair up and sat. "You've been to the center?"

"Yes. You and your family are to be congratulated. It's wonderful."

"Then you'll agree to have your company perform?"

"I'll agree to negotiate a contract." Eve pulled the back of her chaise up so that she could settle into a sitting position. "The facilities are first class. If we can iron out the details, we'll both have what we want."

"Such details are for lawyers and accountants," he said in dismissal. "We need only agree on what is to be done."

Though she thought her father would have been amused by his attitude toward accountants, she folded her hands. "We'll agree after the lawyers and accountants have had their say."

"It appears you've become a businesswoman."

"It doesn't just appear, I have. Don't you approve of women in business, Your Highness?"

"Cordina is a forward-looking country. We don't approve or disapprove on the basis of gender."

"The royal 'we,'" she murmured under her breath. "I'm sure that's very progressive. Aren't you roasting in that jacket?"

"There's a breeze."

"Don't you ever unbutton your collar or take off your shoes?"

"I beg your pardon?"

"Never mind. You're too literal." She lifted a glass filled with citrus punch from the table beside her. The ice had melted, but it was still refreshing. "Do you ever use the pool, Your Highness?"

"When time permits."

"Ever hear the American saying about all work and no play?"

He sat coolly in the baking sun, the gold-and-ruby ring on his finger glinted. His eyes were shadowed. "I believe I have."

"But it doesn't apply to princes?"

"I apologize for not being able to entertain you."

"I don't need entertainment." Frustrated, she rose. When he stood, she spun on him. "Oh sit, will you? It's only the two of us. Don't you think women get tired of having a man pop up everytime they do?"

Alexander settled again, surprised to find himself amused. "No."

"Well, they do. It might do you some good to spend more time in America, learning how to unbend."

"I'm not in a position to unbend," he said quietly and Eve felt her temper ease away.

"All right, though I can't understand why that's true with a friend of the family. You'll have to excuse me, Your Highness. I've little patience with unnecessary formality."

"Then why don't you ever call me by my name?" His question had her turning to face him again, frowning and uncomfortable. "You said yourself, we've known each other for years."

"I was wrong." She said it slowly, sensing something under the surface. "We don't know each other at all."

"You have no trouble addressing the other members of my family by their name rather than their title."

She wished for her drink again, but found herself unable to cross near him to get it. "No, I don't."

"It causes me to ask myself why." With his eyes on hers, he rose and walked to her. When they were close, face to face, he stopped, but kept his hands at his side. "Or perhaps I should ask you why."

"It never seemed appropriate, that's all."

Nerves? He'd never seen nerves in her before. Intrigued, he stepped closer. "Have I been unfriendly?"

"Yes—no." She caught herself taking a step back.

"Which is it?"

"No." She stood firm and called herself a fool. "You're always polite, Your Highness. I know you've never approved of me, but—"

"I've given that impression?"

He was closer again. She hadn't even seen him move. Eve fell back on the only defense at hand. Belligerence. "Loud and clear."

"Then I should apologize." He took her hand and brought it to his lips. Eve wondered why she should hear thunder when the sky was so clear.

"Don't be charming." She tried to tug her hand away and found it firmly caught.

His smile was as unexpected as the kiss on her fingers, and just as weakening. Yes, she was nervous. He found the unforeseen vulnerability irresistible. "You prefer rudeness?"

"I prefer the expected."

"So do I." Something came and went in his eyes quickly. If it was a challenge, she promised herself it was one she would never answer. "It isn't always there. And from time to time, the unexpected is more interesting."

"Interesting for some, uncomfortable for others."

His smile deepened. She saw for the first time a small dimple at the side of his mouth. For some reason her gaze seemed locked to it. "Do I make you uncomfortable, Eve?"

"I didn't say that." She tore her gaze from his mouth, but found meeting his eyes wasn't any less unnerving.

"Your face is flushed," he murmured, and stroked a thumb along her cheek.

"It's the heat," she managed, then felt her knees tremble when his gaze locked on hers.

"I believe you're right." He felt it, too, sizzling in the air, crackling, like an electric storm over the sea. "The wise thing for both of us is to cool off."

"Yes. I have to change. I told Bennett I'd go down to the stables with him before dinner."

Alexander withdrew immediately. Whatever she thought she had seen in his face, in his eyes, was gone. "I'll let you go, then. The French ambassador and his wife will be joining us for dinner."

"I'll try not to slurp my soup."

Temper, always close to the surface, came into his eyes. "Are you making fun of me, Eve, or yourself?"

"Both."

"Don't stay in the sun much longer." He turned and didn't look back.

Eve watched him stride away in his strong, military gait. She shivered once, then shut her eyes and dove headlong into the pool.

Eve was relieved to find not only Bennett but Brie and Reeve joining them at dinner. Seated between the ambassador and Reeve, she found herself saved from having to make the obligatory dinner conversation with Alexander. As heir, he sat at the head of the table, flanked by his sister on one side and the ambassador's wife on the other.

The dinner was formal but not, as Eve had feared, unbearably boring. The ambassador had a wealth of anecdotes, any of which he would expound on given the least encouragement. Eve laughed with him, urged him on, then delighted him by carrying on a conversation in French. Her years in the Swiss school had stuck, whether she'd wanted them to or not.

"Impressive," Reeve toasted her when she turned to him with a grin. He'd changed little over the years, she thought. There was a touch of gray at the temples, but that was all. No, she corrected, that wasn't all. He was more relaxed now. Happiness, it seemed, was its own fountain of youth.

"How's your French coming?"

"It isn't." He toyed with the rich duck in its delicate sauce and thought how much he would have preferred a steak, rare, cooked over his own grill. Then he glanced over at his wife as she laughed with Bennett. Whatever sacrifices had been made were nothing compared to the rewards. "Gabriella says I'm determined not to learn."

"And?"

"She's right."

Eve laughed and picked up her wine. "I'm looking forward to seeing your farm tomorrow, Reeve. Chris told me the house was lovely, though she got lost when you started in on wheat or oats. And you have horses."

"All the children ride. Even Dorian sits on a pony." He paused as the main course was cleared. "It's amazing how fast they learn."

"How does it feel?" She turned a little more, not certain where the question had come from or why it seemed so important. "Living here, I mean, or living here most of the year, having to sink down another set of roots, learn new customs?"

He could have passed it off as some men would. He could have made a joke as others might. But he had a fondness for the truth. "It was difficult at first, for both of us. Now it's home. Just as Virginia's home. I can't say I won't be happy when Alex marries and Brie has fewer obligations, but I fell in love with the woman. Her rank is part of it, part of her."

"It is more than just a title, isn't it?" she murmured. Before she realized it, before she could prevent it, her gaze drifted to Alexander.

"A great deal more," Reeve agreed, aware of where her interest had shifted. "And more yet for him."

Eve brought her attention back quickly. "Yes, of course. He'll rule one day."

"He's been molded for it from his first breath." Were Gabriella's instincts right? Reeve wondered. Was there a spark between Alexander and Eve that would take very little fanning. He'd never seen it, but tonight he wasn't so sure. If there was, Eve wouldn't find it an easy road. Reeve mulled over his wine a moment, then kept his voice quiet. "If there's one thing I've learned in the past few years, it's that duty and obligation aren't choices for some, or for the people who love them."

He was telling her what she already knew, and more than she wanted to know. "No, I'm sure you're right." To ease the tension that had come so quickly, she turned to the ambassador and made him laugh.

The dinner party moved to the main parlor with coffee and brandy. Calculating that a decent amount of time had elapsed, Bennett took Eve's hand. "Air," he whispered in her ear.

"Rude," she whispered back.

"No, they'll talk for an hour yet. And I'm entitled, even obliged, to entertain you as well as the others. Let's just step out on the terrace."

The invitation was hard to resist. Eve already knew how tempting nights in Cordina were. A quick glance showed her that Alexander had the ambassador engaged in quiet conversation and that Brie and Reeve were dealing with the ambassador's wife.

"All right. For a minute."

Though his flow of words never faltered, Alexander saw Eve move with his brother through the terrace doors.

"Better," Bennett said immediately.

"It was a lovely dinner."

"It was fine, but sometimes I'd prefer pizza and beer with a few friends." He walked to the edge and leaned on a low stone wall. "The older I get, the less time there is for it."

"It isn't easy, is it?"

"What?"

"Being who you are."

He swung an arm around her waist. "It has its moments."

"No, don't shrug it off. You always do that." Eve drew back to study him. He was wonderful to look at and tougher, a great deal tougher, than he allowed himself to seem.

"You want a serious answer." He dipped his hands into his pockets. "It's difficult to give you one. I've always been who I am, what I am. No, it isn't always easy to know that wherever you go there's a bodyguard not far behind or the press not far ahead. I deal with it in my own way. I'm permitted to, as Brie is, to a certain extent. We're not the heir."

"Do you wish you were?"

"God, no."

He said it with such speed and force she had to smile. "There's not a jealous bone in your body, is there?"

"It's hardly a matter of envy. As long as I can remember, Alex has had to work harder, study harder. Be harder. No, I wouldn't step into his shoes. Why do you ask?"

"Oh, I don't know. The American fascination with royalty, I suppose."

"You've known us too long to be fascinated."

"I've known some of you." With a shake of her head, she walked to him. "Do you remember that first night, the night of the ball, when we walked out on one of those high, dark balconies?"

"That's hardly a night I'd forget."

"I was fascinated then. I thought you were going to kiss me."

He grinned and twined a lock of her hair around his finger. "I never got around to it."

"No, you ended up getting shot, instead. I thought you were very heroic."

"I was." He linked his arms loosely around her waist. "You know, if I tried to kiss you now, I'd feel as though I were making a pass at my sister."

"I know." Relaxed, she rested her head on his shoulder. "I'm glad we're friends, Ben."

"You wouldn't happen to have a cousin, a half sister, an aunt, who looks anything like you?"

"Sorry." Smiling, she tilted her head back to look at him.

"Me, too."

"Bennett."

It only took Alexander's voice to have Eve springing back like a child caught in the cookie jar. She cursed herself for it, then balled her hands into fists at her side.

"Excuse me." Coolly regal, he stood just outside the terrace doors where the moonlight didn't reach. "The ambassador is leaving."

"So soon?" Untouched by the biting tone, Bennett squeezed Eve's shoulder's. "Well, we should make our good-byes. Thanks for the air."

"Of course." But as he walked through the doors, she stayed where she was, hoping Alexander would follow him.

"If you'd come back in for a moment, the ambassador would like to say good-bye. He was quite charmed by you at dinner."

"All right." She walked to the doors, but found her way blocked. This time she didn't step back, but angled her chin so she could see his face. It was in shadows, and only his eyes were clear. "Was there something else, Your Highness?"

"Yes, it seems there is." He caught her chin in his hand, surprising both of them. It was soft, with the pressure still a threat or a promise. It wasn't a lover's touch. He refused to allow it to be. "Bennett is a generous man, a compassionate one, but a man who has little discretion with women. You should take care."

From someone else, from anyone else, the comment would have made her laugh. Meeting Alexander's eyes, she didn't feel like laughing. "It appears you're warning me I might get burned again. It wasn't necessary this afternoon and it isn't necessary now." Her voice was slow and sultry, but somehow managed to take on the sheen of ice. "You might have observed, Your Highness, that American women insist on taking care of themselves and making their own choices.''

''I have no desire to take care of you.'' There was a sting in his voice that might have made her shrivel if she hadn't been so angry.

''We can all be grateful for that.''

''If you're in love with my brother—''

''What right do you have to ask me that?'' Eve demanded. She didn't know why the temper had come or why it was so fierce, but with every word it grew. ''My feelings for your brother are *my* feelings and have nothing to do with you.''

The words twisted inside him hatefully. ''He is my brother.''

''You don't rule Bennett and you certainly don't rule me. My feelings for your brother, or for anyone, are my business.''

''What happens in my home, in my family, is mine.''

''Alex.'' Brie came to the door, her voice subdued to indicate theirs weren't. ''The ambassador's waiting.''

Without a word he dropped his hand and strode inside.

''Your brother's an idiot,'' Eve said under her breath.

''In a great many ways.'' Sympathetic, Brie took Eve's hand. ''Take a deep breath and come in and speak to the ambassador and his wife a moment. Then you can go up to your room and kick something. That's what I always do.''

Eve set her teeth. ''Thanks. I believe I will.''

Chapter Three

PRINCE BENNETT COURTS AMERICAN HEIRESS.

Eve read the headline with her morning coffee and nearly choked. Once she managed to swallow and take a second look, she began to giggle. Poor Ben, she thought, all he had to do was look at a woman and there was a romance. Ignoring her croissant, Eve read the text:

Eve Hamilton, daughter of millionaire T. G. Hamilton, is the guest of the royal family during her visit to Cordina. The long and intimate connection between Prince Bennett and Miss Hamilton began seven years ago...

The article went on to describe the events that took place in the palace resulting in the abortive kidnapping of the princess and Bennett's subsequent injuries. She couldn't help but smile when her own part was played up heroically. Amused, she read that she and Bennett had enjoyed periodic rendezvous over the years.

Rendezvous, she thought with a snicker. Well, it was true that Bennett had come to Houston to help her celebrate her twenty-first birthday. One of her closest friends had fallen madly in love with him for about a week. Because of the connection, she'd been asked to accompany him on a tour of Washington a few years before. And she had visited Cordina a few times with her sister. Then there was the time she and Bennett had hooked up in Paris quite by accident. It was difficult to think of one lunch in a public café as a rendezvous, but the press needed to print something.

"Will another member of the royal family choose an American?"

The article ended with the question. Don't hold your breath, she answered silently, then set the paper aside. What would the press have to talk about when Bennett did meet the right woman and settle? Laughing to herself, she picked up her cooling croissant. By then it was very likely Brie's children would be old enough to marry.

"Interesting reading?"

Eve glanced over at the entrance of the little solarium. She should have known he wouldn't let her have breakfast in peace. "I enjoy a joke, Your Highness." She started to rise, when he waved her back into her seat.

"You consider this funny?"

"I got a laugh out of it, though I imagine Ben gets tired of having every woman he smiles at added to the list of prospective wives."

"He thinks little of it." As, under most circumstances, Alexander did himself. "Ben enjoys a scandal."

Because it was said without heat, she smiled. If he wanted to let the words exchanged the night before be forgotten, she was more than willing. She'd spent long enough stewing about them. "Who doesn't?" At a closer glance he looked tired, and more than a little strained. Sympathetic, she softened. "Have you had breakfast? I can offer you coffee and croissants."

"Yes, a few hours ago. I could use the coffee."

She rose and took another cup and saucer from the server. "It's barely ten, but you look as though you've had a difficult day."

For a moment he said nothing. Such was his training. Then he relented. It would be on the radio and in the papers soon enough. "There was news from Paris this morning. A bomb at the embassy."

Her fingers tightened on the handle of the coffeepot. "Oh, God, your father."

"He's not hurt. His secretary was injured slightly." He paused, but his voice was calm and even when he continued. "Seward, the assistant to the minister, was killed."

"I'm sorry." She set down the pot to put a hand on his arm. "I'm so sorry. Do they know who did it?"

"No one's taken the credit. We have only suspicions."

"Is the prince coming home?"

He looked through the glass to where the sun was bright and the flowers blooming. Life would never be just that simple, he reminded himself. Never just that ordinary. "The business in Paris isn't completed."

"But—"

"He'll come home when it is." He lifted his cup and drank the coffee black and steaming. "Cordina, like many other countries, takes a strong stand against terrorism. They will be found."

"I hope so." She pushed the flaky croissant aside and found the headline no longer amused her. "Why is it so many innocents pay for the politics of others?"

His fingers tightened on the cup, part in fury, part in frustration. "There are no politics in terrorism."

"No." There was a great deal she didn't understand and more she would have liked to close her eyes on. But she knew that burying one's head in the sand did nothing but put grit in one's eyes. "No, you're right, of course."

"Seward leaves a wife and three children."

"Oh, how awful. Have they been told?"

"I have to go tell them now."

"Can I help? I could go with you."

"It's not your affair."

Eve retreated, calling herself a fool for being hurt. When he rose, she stared down into her coffee and said nothing.

Why had he come here? Alexander asked himself. He'd needed to tell her, to share his frustration, his anger, his grief. It wasn't wise for a man who had to rule to need comfort, a soft word, a hand to hold. He'd been taught to rely on himself, yet he'd come to her. And he still needed.

"Eve." It wasn't easy for him. She couldn't know that a simple request set off a violent tug-of-war inside him. "It would help if you went with me. I think she could use a woman."

"I'll get my purse," was all she said.

The Sewards lived in a pretty pink stucco house with a small, neat lawn bordered by white flowers. Eve saw a red bike in the drive. It was that more than anything that clutched at her heart. She knew what it was like to lose a parent, and that the hurt and grief never completely healed over.

Alexander offered his hand after he stepped from the car. Eve accepted it, then let hers remain there.

"If you're uncomfortable—"

"No. No, only sad." She walked with him to the door, aware that the driver watched them, but unaware that members of the security staff were stationed up and down the quiet street.

Alena Seward opened the door herself. She was a dark, plump woman of early middle age with lovely eyes and mussed hair. It was obvious they had caught her in the middle of cleaning. Her mouth dropped open the moment she saw Alexander, but she recovered quickly.

"Your Highness."

"Madame Seward, I apologize for coming to your home unexpectedly. May we come in?"

"Of course." Eve saw her eyes shift to the furniture that had yet to be dusted, to toys that had yet to be tidied. "May I offer you coffee, Your Highness?"

"No, thank you. May I present Miss Eve Hamilton."

"How do you do?" The woman offered a hand. "Please sit down."

Alexander took a chair, knowing the woman would remain standing if he did. "Madame Seward, there was news from Paris this morning."

Seated beside Alena on the sofa, Eve felt the other woman tense. "Yes, Your Highness."

"Two bombs were planted at our embassy. One detonated before it was discovered." He knew from experience that bad news, the worst news, was best given quickly. "Your husband was killed."

"Maurice?" Her fingers tightened on Eve's hand, though she was unaware that it had been offered. "Dead?"

"He was killed instantly, *madame*. My father sends his grief and his condolences, and I and the rest of my family give ours."

"There is a mistake?" There were no tears, but the fingers around Eve's hand were like clamps.

He hated the helplessness more than anything else. He could give her no hope, and sympathy was such an empty gift. "No, *madame*. He was alone in the office when it exploded."

"Brandy." Eve forced Alena's attention to her. "Madame Seward, where is your brandy?"

"Brandy?" Her voice was as blank as her eyes. "There is brandy in the kitchen."

Eve only looked at Alexander. He rose and went to find it himself.

"But I spoke to him just yesterday," Alena murmured. "He was well—tired. The meetings drag on so long. He'd bought a little jeweled pin for our daughter. Her birthday is next month." On this her voice began to quiver. "There's a mistake. *Mademoiselle?*"

Then the tears came. Eve did the only thing she knew how. She held. When Alexander entered the room again Eve had the widow's head on her breast. Her own eyes were overflowing as she stroked Alena's hair. Grief filled the room, replacing disbelief. In a movement that had nothing to do with protocol and everything to do with compassion, he knelt in front of them and urged the brandy on Alena.

"You have a sister, *madame*," he said gently. "Would you like me to phone her now?"

"My children."

"I'll have them brought home."

She took a shaky sip of brandy. "I would like my sister, Your Highness."

"Where is your phone?"

"In the office. Maurice's office, down the hall." She turned back into Eve's shoulder and wept.

"You were very kind," Alexander said when they were back in his car.

Eve shut her eyes, leaning her head back against the seat. "Kindness often doesn't seem to be enough."

He could say nothing to that. He'd felt the same. Why when he carried the burden of power was there so little he could do?

"What will happen to her?"

"She and her children will be provided for. We can do that." He pulled out a cigarette. The taste in his mouth was already harsh. "We can't heal the wounds."

She heard it in his voice, the bitterness tinged with frustration. For the first time, she thought she really understood. "You want to punish someone."

He lit the cigarette, then turned to see her eyes open and on him. "I will punish someone."

The way he said it had Eve's mouth going dry. He had the power, not only in his title, not only in his birthright. If he'd been born a peasant, he'd have had it still. Maybe it was this above everything else that kept her drawn toward him even as she inched away.

"When you were on the phone, Alena asked me who had done it. I had to tell her I didn't know, but I know she'll ask again, when the grief eases."

"When the grief passes there comes a hunger for revenge."

"You want that."

"It could have been my father." For the first time, she saw his control slip. It dangled dangerously a moment, showing in the heat and fury of his eyes, before he ripped it back. "We are responsible to our country, to our people. Seward's death will not be ignored."

"You believe the bomb was planted for your father?" She reached out to take his wrist. "It was meant for him?"

"It was planted in his office. It was only coincidence that he was called away moments before the explosion. Had he not, he would have died with Seward."

"Then that's all the more reason he should come home."

"That's all the more reason he must stay. If a ruler is intimidated, his country is intimidated."

"Damn it, he's your father."

"He is Armand of Cordina first."

"You don't believe that. You don't really feel that way." The intensity was in her voice, in her fingers as they gripped his flesh. "If your father's in danger, you have to convince him to come back."

"If he were to ask my advice, I would tell him that to return to Cordina before his business is completed would be a mistake."

She withdrew slowly until they were no longer touching. "Bennett said you were hard, had to be hard. I wonder if he meant this much." When the car pulled up at the palace steps, she was out before him. "For a moment back at that house, I thought I saw something in you, warmth, humanity. I should have known better. You have no feelings, because you have no heart."

He caught her arm before she reached the door. "You understand nothing. I'm under no obligation to explain myself to you or to anyone." Yet he had a need to. The man inside the title desperately needed her understanding. "A man is dead, a good man, an honest man, a man I hunted with, gambled with. His wife is left with her grief and the grief of her children and I can do nothing. Nothing."

He tossed her arm aside, then strode back down the stairs. Eve watched him disappear into the side garden.

For a moment she stood where she was, breathing hard, close to tears. She took a deep breath, another, then went after him.

This woman, damn her, was making him forget who he was, what he had to be. There was a distance that had to be maintained between his feelings and his obligation, between the man and his title. With his family, in private, it could be different. Even with his closest friends the reserve had to be put into place when necessary. He couldn't afford to allow himself the luxury of being too—what had she said—human, when the responsibility was so great. More now than ever.

He'd lost a valued friend, and for what? Because of some vague and violent statement by a nameless group of terrorists. No, he didn't believe that. He tore a blossom from a bush as he passed. A man was more than a stalk to be broken on a whim. There had been a purpose, and Seward had been a mistake.

His father had been the target. Alexander was as sure of that as he was of his own name. And Deboque, the animal, had been the trigger.

"Your Highness."

He turned and saw Eve. The garden flowered around her, ripe, lush and tropical. It suited her name, he thought, as she did. But with the first Eve it had been the fruit that had been forbidden, not the woman.

"I want to apologize." She said it quickly. For her, apologies, like mistakes, were easier to swallow than to speak.

"When I'm wrong, I'm often very wrong. I hope you'll believe that I'm sorry."

"I believe you're sorry, Eve, just as I believe you meant what you said."

She opened her mouth to contradict, then shut it again. "I guess that has to do for both of us."

He studied her a moment, aware she was still angry, and angrier still that her conscience had forced her to apologize. It was something he understood perhaps too well, the frustration of having a temper and being forced to restrain it. "A peace offering," he decided on impulse, and offered her the flower. "It doesn't sit well with me to have been rude to a guest."

She took the blossom, breathing in the light tang of vanilla while she struggled not to be charmed. "It would be all right to be rude if I weren't a guest?"

"You're very blunt."

"Yes." Then she smiled and tucked the flower behind her ear. "Lucky for both of us I'm not one of your subjects."

"That's something we won't argue about." He looked up at the sky, as clear and perfect a blue as could be wished for. She saw the strain, the sorrow, and was moved to reach out one more time.

"Is it only permitted for you to mourn in private, Your Highness?"

He looked at her again. There was compassion there, an offering of friendship. For so long he'd forbidden himself to accept even that much from her. But there was a weight on him, a desperately heavy one. He closed his eyes a moment and made a quick negative move with his head.

"He was closer to my father's age than mine, yet he was one of the few people I could talk with freely. Maurice had no pretentions, none of the sharp edges ambition often gives us."

"He was your friend." She came closer, and before he realized her intention, had wrapped her arms around him. "I hadn't understood he was your friend. I'm so sorry."

She was killing him by inches with her warmth, her understanding. He needed more, too much more. His hands rested lightly on her shoulders when he burned to skim them over her to bring her closer. The scent of her hair, of her skin, raced through his system, but he could do no more than stand and be assaulted.

He'd been trained to fight, to defend, to protect, yet he was defenseless. Flowers spread out, curtaining them from the palace, but there could be no haven for a man who coveted what belonged to his brother.

It hurt. He knew that beneath the title, beyond the position, he was flesh and blood, but it was rare to experience pain this sharp and sweet. It tangled with the grief and the anger until it threatened to explode in a passion he would be helpless to control. Feelings released weren't as easily ignored as feelings restrained.

He drew away abruptly and his eyes were cool and distant.

"I have a great deal to see to." The struggle with desire made his voice curt and his manner stiff. "You'll have to excuse me. I'll see if Bennett is available to join you for lunch."

And he was gone while she could only stand and stare after him.

Didn't he feel anything? Eve demanded. Couldn't he? Was he so empty of normal feelings that he hadn't been affected when her insides had turned to jelly? For a moment she'd thought ... She'd been a fool to think, she told herself, but found a small stone bench because her knees had begun to tremble. A fool to think he'd felt that need, that longing, that crystal-clear rightness when their bodies had touched.

She'd meant the gesture for comfort, but the moment it had been made her world had turned upside down. She'd wanted to go on just standing there with her cheek close to his, saying nothing, feeling everything. But that wasn't what *he* had felt, she thought, and closed her eyes. She was letting her reach exceed her grasp.

Alexander of Cordina wasn't for her. She should thank God for that, because it would be terrifying if he were. A sane woman might dream of loving a prince, but that same woman would be wise to remember that her choices would diminish if she did, her privacy would end altogether and her chances for a normal life would be nil. Beyond that, the man himself was frightening enough. He wouldn't be kind unless the mood suited him, and he would never be patient. A man like Alexander expected perfection, while she respected flaws.

Yet she'd wanted him. For one mad moment, she'd forgotten who and what he was, and had wanted to be held, to be loved by him. Would the world change somehow if she were loved by him? In the garden, with the scent of wisteria floating over her head, she thought it might. Yet she'd wanted to be the one to take that strained, weary look from around his eyes and make him smile again.

It would pass, Eve assured herself. She was too practical to indulge herself in foolish fantasies. And if it didn't pass naturally, she would push it along. She had work to concentrate on, plays to produce, a company to organize.

First thing in the morning, she'd be leaving Cordina. By the time she returned, any momentary insanity would be forgotten, and she'd be too busy to indulge in any more.

Not entirely reassured, she rose. At least her legs were solid again. She'd try to find Bennett. Nothing and no one would clear her head faster.

"I can't believe what you've done with this place, Brie." Eve sat on the wide, shady veranda and looked out at the long, rolling lawn, the paddocks, the acres of turned and tended earth. The youngest child, Dorian, sat at the bottom of the steps and fondled a new kitten.

"There are times I can't, either." Gabriella turned her head to see her elder children kicking a ball through the grass. "I'd always hoped for this without ever really believing it. I was pregnant with Kristian when we broke ground for the house, so it's five years now. When we brought him home, we brought him here."

"Only five," Eve mused. "When I look at the house, it's as though it had been here forever."

"For the children it has." The kitten let out a squeal. "Dorian, be gentle."

He looked up, a miniature of his father, and grinned wickedly, but his small, curious hands petted the kitten's fur easily. "Purrs," he said, pleased with himself.

"Yes, and if you pull his ears, he'll scratch."

"It's wonderful here in the evening." Eve watched the sun hang low over the newly planted fields. There were two servants inside, a fraction of what the palace used. The smells of cooking came through the windows, rich and homey, as suited the country. "Is this like your home in Virginia?"

"The house is older there." Gabriella took her eyes off her son long enough to watch Reeve, Alexander and Bennett circle the barn. She knew what they were talking about. The bomb in Paris was on everyone's mind. She and Reeve would talk of it later. Now she turned back to Eve. "It seems we're always fixing something—the roof, the windows. I'm afraid we don't spend as much time there as Reeve would like."

"Brie, you don't have to make conversation with me. I know you're concerned about your father and what happened this morning."

"These are uneasy times." Brie looked at her children again. They were her heart, her life, her continuing link with the real world. "We have to live each day. I know my father will do what's right for Cordina."

"And for himself?"

Gabriella's eyes, a deep, intriguing topaz, seemed to darken, but she smiled. "My father is Cordina, as Alex is. It's the first thing that has to be understood, and the most difficult. You care for him."

"For Alexander? Of course."

"Of course." Amused, Gabriella rose to pick up her son before he could crawl under the porch after the kitten. "I'm not speaking of 'of course,' Eve." She kissed Dorian on the cheek when he started to squirm, then settled him expertly on her hip. "If you ever allow your feelings for him to come to the surface, you'll find a great many pitfalls. If you need to talk, come to me." Then she laughed when Dorian tugged on her hair. "This one needs a good wash before dinner."

"Go ahead." Eve managed to smile. "I'll get the others."

But she sat there alone a few moments longer, not so sure of herself and no longer relaxed. Her feelings for Alexander were on the surface, she told herself. She cared about him as she cared about all the friends she'd made in Cordina. They were like a second family to her. Naturally, as a woman she found Alexander attractive. What woman wouldn't? And perhaps there were moments, occasionally, when the attraction was a little too intense. That was nothing to lose sleep over.

She didn't want pitfalls. She'd maneuver them if she had to. In her career. Romantically—that was a different area altogether. She wanted no complications there. Wasn't that the reason she had avoided romance for so long? Certainly there'd been men who had interested her, but . . .

There'd always been a "but," Eve thought. Rather than think it through too deeply, she'd always fallen back on the fact that she simply didn't have time for relationships.

The noise of the children shouting roused her. It wasn't like her to daydream, either, she reminded herself. Jogging down the steps, she headed across the lawn. The children groaned a bit, but, after she promised to help them organize a game after dinner, went in to wash up.

With them gone, the farm was so quiet she almost regretted having to find the others and go inside. She'd like to come back, Eve discovered. To sit on the porch in the evening, close her eyes and listen to nothing. It wouldn't do for every day, even every week, but now and again it would be like healing oneself.

She enjoyed the frantic pace of the life she'd chosen. Eve could go for days with little sleep and no spare time and not feel the strain. But once a year, twice a year, perhaps, to sit in the country and listen to nothing... Laughing at herself, she headed for the barn.

There were high windows to let in the evening light, and the scent of horses was strong. No stranger to barns and stables, Eve headed down the sloping concrete floor. She squinted a bit, trying to adjust her vision to the change in light.

"Bennett, I—"

But it was Alexander who turned. The figure she had seen in front of the stall was darker and slightly broader than Bennett.

"Excuse me, Your Highness." Her manner stiffened automatically. "I thought you were Bennett."

"I'm aware of that. He's with Reeve." Alexander turned back to the horse. "They've gone to look at the new bull."

"Dinner's almost ready. I told your sister—oh, she's lovely, isn't she?" Distracted by the mare, Eve stepped closer to stroke. "By the time Brie took me on a tour of the house, I'd forgotten I'd wanted to see the horses. Yes, you're lovely," Eve murmured, and ran her fingers down the mare's nose. "Does she have a name?"

"Spot," he said, and watched Eve laugh.

"What a name for a horse."

"I gave her to Adrienne as a birthday gift. She thought it was a fine name." He nuzzled the mare's ears. "We didn't have the heart to make her change it."

"She's lovely in any case. I named my first horse Sir Lancelot. I suppose I was more fanciful than Adrienne."

He lifted a hand to stroke the horse alongside hers. Their fingers trailed down but never touched. "Strange, I never saw you as the type for knights in shining armor."

"I was six, and I—" The rest was cut off as the mare gave Eve's shoulder a hard push and sent her tumbling against Alexander. "I beg your pardon, Your Highness."

"'Alex,' damn it." She was in his arms as she had been that afternoon. It was too late to prepare, too late to stem the feelings that rose up in him. "My name is Alexander. Must you insist on making me feel like a position instead of a man?"

"I don't mean to. I'm sorry." It was washing over her again, that warm giddy feeling. A storm brewing. Water rising. She didn't pull away. Her intellect told her to pull away and pull away quickly. She had no business being with him like this. Alone. Listening to nothing.

His fingers crept into her hair, tangled there. Trapped. "Is it so difficult to think of me as flesh and blood?"

"No, I—yes." She couldn't get her breath. The air in the barn was suddenly sultry, stifling. "I have to find Bennett."

"Not this time." He pulled her close, damning who he was. "Say my name. Now."

There was gold in his eyes. Flecks of it. She'd never seen it before, never allowed herself to. Now, as the light grew dimmer, she could see nothing else. "Alexander." She only breathed his name. Heat flowed through him like lava.

"Again."

"Alexander," she whispered, then pressed her mouth desperately to his.

It was everything she'd wanted. Everything she'd waited for. She heard the thunder, felt the lightning, tasted the heat finally escaped. With no thought to place, to time, to position, she wrapped her arms around him and let her body absorb.

There was no cool control here, not the kind he coated himself with. She'd known it would be different, somehow she'd always known. His mouth was open, urgent, as if he had waited all of his life for this one moment. She felt his fingers dig into her flesh and trembled at the knowledge that she could be wanted so forcefully.

He forgot everything but that he was tasting her at last. She was hot, spicy, aggressive. She'd been born for the tropics, for steamy days and steamy nights. Her hair flowed down her back, through his fingers. He gripped it as though it were a line to safety, though he knew the woman was danger.

His tongue dove deeper to taste, to tease, to tempt. She was an aphrodisiac, and he was mindless with her flavor. Her hands were running over his back, kneading the muscles. He wanted them on his flesh where he could feel each stroke, each scrape.

The air in the barn carried the scent of animal. Each moment his lips were on hers, he lost a bit more of the civilized. He wanted her there, while the sun went down and the barn became dark and quiet with night.

"Eve?" The barn door creaked open, letting in a thin, dusky stream of light. "Did you get lost in here?"

Head swimming, Eve leaned back against the wall and tried to catch her breath. "No. No, Bennett, we'll be right in." She pressed a hand to her throat.

"Hurry along, will you? I'm starved." The barn door shut and the light was lost.

He'd nearly been lost, Alexander thought. Lost in her, lost to her. What right did she have to make him ache and want and need? She was standing there now, silent, her eyes dark and huge. How could a woman look so innocent when she'd nearly destroyed a man's soul?

"You change allegiance easily, Eve."

Her lips parted, first in confusion, then in surprise. The hurt came quickly, but before it could make her weak, she let in the fury. Her hand swept out and came hard against his face. The slap echoed, then silence remained.

"I'm sure you can have me deported for that at the very least." There was no hitch in her voice because she fought it down. There was only ice. "Just remember, if you decide to have me dragged away in irons, Your Highness, you deserved that. That and one hell of a lot more.''

Fighting the need to run away, she turned and walked out of the barn as regally as one born to it.

He didn't go after her. His temper pushed him to, to go for her, to punish her somehow in some way. Not for the slap—that had been a small thing. But her words, the look in her eyes had carried more sting. What right did she have to make him feel remorse, to make him feel guilt, when it was she who had turned from one brother to the next without a qualm?

But he wanted her. He wanted his brother's woman with a desperation that was slowly eating him alive.

He'd always wanted her, Alexander admitted as he rammed the side of his fist into the wall. The horses whinnied nervously, then settled. He'd always fought it. He ran a hand over his face, fighting to recapture the composure that was an essential part of his position.

He would fight it still, he promised himself. Love for his brother left him no choice. But he could damn the woman, he thought grimly as he strode out of the barn. And he did.

Chapter Four

"You come and go so much these days I never get to see you."

Eve folded her oldest and most serviceable sweats in her suitcase before she glanced at her sister. "Things have been crazy. They're going to get crazier."

"You've been back from Cordina for two months, and I've talked to your phone machine more than I have to you." Chris dropped on the edge of the bed and studied the sapphire-colored silk blouse Eve packed beside the sweats. She started to suggest tissue paper, then reminded herself that baby sister had grown up.

Both sisters had dark, thick hair, but Eve's was pulled back in a braid, while Chris wore her hair chin-length and swingy. The family resemblance was there, in the shadowy cheekbones, the milky skin. It wasn't age that separated them so much as style. Chris had a polish that had come from years of dealing with the art world and those wealthy enough to indulge themselves with art. Eve had a sensuality that she wore as casually as another woman wore scent. Once it had given the elder sister a great deal of worry. Now Chris could simply marvel at it.

"Now you're going off again. I guess if I want to see my sister, I'll have to do it in Cordina."

"I was hoping you would." Eve tucked a small leather cosmetic case in the side of her Pullman. "I hate to admit it, but I'm going to need all the moral support I can drum up."

"Nervous?" Chris circled her knee with linked hands. "You?"

"Nervous. Me. I've never taken on anything this big. Four plays." She checked the contents of her briefcase for the third time. "Hauling actors, technicians, assistants, seamstresses to the Mediterranean, dumping them in front of an international audience and claiming that we represent the American theater." She pulled out a notebook, flipped through it, then stuck it back in her briefcase. "That's a hell of a boast."

"Too late for cold feet," Chris said briskly. She brushed dark, feathered bangs back from her forehead. "Besides, the Hamilton Company of Players is an American theater group, isn't it?"

"Yes, but—"

"And you'll be performing American plays, right?"

"Right. Still—"

"No stills, no buts." A trio of rings glinted on Chris's hand as she waved Eve's words away. "You *are* representing American theater. And you're going to be fantastic."

"See." Eve leaned over the suitcase to kiss Chris's cheek. "That's why I need you."

"I'll do my best to work my schedule so I can be there for the first performance. Even though I know you'll be too busy to do more than blink at me."

"I promise to do more than that. Hopefully after the first performance, I'll settle down." She folded a pair of slacks by the pleats, then smoothed them carefully into the case. "It's the preparation and paperwork that has me edgy."

"You've Daddy's knack for handling details, a fact that constantly amazes me." Still, Chris had to restrain herself from asking Eve if she had her passport. "I don't doubt you're going to pull this thing off without a hitch."

Had she packed the red suit? Eve started to check one more time, then forced herself to stop. She'd packed it. She'd packed everything. "I wish you were going with me so you could tell me that at regular intervals."

"The Bissets trust you. This wouldn't be happening otherwise. I might not be there for the next few weeks, but you'll have Brie behind you, and Alex and Bennett."

Eve zipped her case closed in one long move. "I don't think I like the idea of having Alexander behind me."

"Still rub you the wrong way?"

"At least. I never get the urge to curtsy and stick out my tongue with Brie or Ben. With him—"

"With him I wouldn't advise it," Chris said with a laugh. "He takes his position too seriously. He has to."

"I suppose."

"Eve, you can't understand what it's like to be the first-born. I can sympathize in a way. The Hamiltons don't have a country, but as far as Daddy's concerned we have an empire." She sighed a bit, knowing her own choices had never quite satisfied him. "Since there was no son to pass the business on to, the pressure fell to me to learn it. When the message finally got across that that wasn't going to work, the pressure changed to my marrying someone who could take over the business. Maybe that's why I've never done either."

"I guess I've never really understood."

"Why should you? It was different for you."

"I know. No pressure here." With a sigh, Eve leaned back against her dresser, taking a last look at the room she wouldn't see for months. "Of course I had to go to school and perform well, and it was expected that I'd restrain myself from doing anything to disgrace the family, but if I'd wanted to sit by the pool for the rest of my life and read magazines, it would have been fine."

"Well, you hid the fact that you had a brain very well."

"I did, didn't I?" She could smile at it now. "From myself, too. In any case, by the time it was discovered, the Hamilton Company of Players was too well established for Daddy to expect me to come into the business. So you're right. I don't really know what it is to be the heir and have little say in my own destiny. Even knowing that, it's difficult for me to feel sorry for Alexander.''

"Oh, I don't know if you should. He's meant to rule as much by personality as by circumstances of birth. I just wish the two of you got along better.'' She took a small white daisy out of a vase on Eve's dresser, broke the stem short, then slipped it into her sister's buttonhole. "You're going to be working closely with him and it isn't going to help if one of you is always making the other snarl.''

Eve took the rest of the flowers out of the vase, wrapped the dripping stems in a tissue and handed them to Chris. "I don't think we'll be working that closely.''

"Isn't Alex president of the center?''

"Presidents delegate,'' she said, and opened her purse to make sure the airline tickets were in place. "Believe me, His Highness doesn't want to work shoulder to shoulder with me anymore than I do with him.'' She closed her purse with a snap. "Probably less.''

"Did something happen when you were out there before?'' Chris rose and put a hand on Eve's hands to keep them still. "You seemed very unnerved when you came back, but I put it down to the project. Now I wonder.''

"You wonder too much,'' Eve told her lightly. "The only thing that happened was that I reaffirmed my belief that Alexander is a pompous, arrogant boor. If this project wasn't so important I'd toss it back in his face and let him sink with it. Just thinking of him makes me angry.''

"Yes, I can see that,'' Chris murmured, and decided to write Gabriella the first chance she had. "Well, if you're lucky, you won't have to deal with him personally.''

"I'm counting on it,'' Eve said with such vehemence that Chris thought it wiser to phone Gabriella the moment her sister was airborne. "It looks like I'm packed. Do I still get that ride to the airport?''

"Absolutely. All we need are three strong men and a pack horse to get your luggage down to the car.''

* * *

Alexander was used to the photographers and reporters, just as he was used to the bodyguards. They had all been a part of his life from birth. Though he'd forced himself not to pace in front of the observation window, he watched the plane land with a vague sense of relief. It had been twenty minutes late and his nerves had begun to stretch.

He hadn't spoken to Eve in weeks. Whatever correspondence had been necessary, whatever details had to be handled, had been seen to through her secretary to his secretary, through his assistant to her assistant. They'd had no contact at all for nearly three months, yet he remembered their few turbulent moments in Gabriella's barn as though they had happened yesterday. If he awoke in the middle of the night, it was the memory of her scent that woke him. If he caught himself daydreaming in the middle of the afternoon, it was her face that had formed in his mind.

He shouldn't think of her at all; yet it was impossible not to. How could he forget the passion and the power that had run through him when he had finally held her? How could he ignore the needs and longings that had burst through him when his mouth had been on hers? He couldn't dismiss her from his mind when, after months had passed, the sensation of her hair tangled in his fingers was so vivid and real.

Work hadn't helped, though he'd heaped it on himself in defense. Worry hadn't helped, though it was there constantly. His father had returned to Cordina. Seward had been buried. Those responsible remained unknown—or unproved. His father's life, his country's well-being, were very much in jeopardy, but he'd yet to erase one woman from his mind. A woman he had no right to desire.

But he did, and desire flared only more strongly when he saw her.

She looked a bit tired, a bit frazzled and very much in charge. Her hair had been braided and clipped on top of her head and she wore large, light-framed sunglasses. As she walked she talked to several people around her while slipping on an oversize red jacket. The rich hue gave her a look of confidence and energy. Alexander realized she'd chosen it for exactly that purpose. She had a briefcase in one hand, a flight bag over her shoulder. In the ten, perhaps fifteen seconds since she had walked into the terminal, he'd noticed every detail.

Her lipstick had worn off, but there was a slight hint of color in her cheeks. The red jacket had gold buttons. A tendril of hair had escaped and curled in front of her left ear. There was a white daisy, a little droopy, in the buttonhole nearest her heart. It made him wonder who had given it to her, who had watched her plane leave, as he'd watched it land.

When she saw him, the slight hint of color disappeared and her shoulders tensed.

She hadn't expected him to be there. She knew, of course, that they were to be met officially, but she hadn't thought it would be Alexander. In her mind she'd planned out the first meeting. She would be rested, refreshed after a long soak in the tub at the hotel. She would have changed into the long, glittery evening gown she'd bought precisely for that purpose. And she would treat him with mild but unmistakable coolness.

Now all she could think was that he was here, looking wonderful. He was so tall, so sturdy. His eyes were so dark, so secretive, they made her want to discover what he hid from everyone else. She wanted to smile, to throw out both hands to him and tell him how good it was to see him. Pride had her sinking into a formal curtsy.

"Your Highness."

He didn't notice the spree of flashbulbs or the crowd of reporters. He was focused on her, on the pout of her lips, on the eyes that met his more in challenge than in greeting.

"Miss Hamilton." He offered his hand. When she hesitated, *because* she hesitated, he brought it deliberately to his lips. Only he was close enough to hear her hiss of breath. "We welcome you and your troupe to Cordina."

Her hand squirmed in his and was held firm. "Thank you, Your Highness."

"Your luggage and transportation are being seen to." He smiled at her, really smiled, with an enjoyment he hadn't felt since she'd left. "Two members of my staff will accompany your troupe to their hotel and see them settled."

Her nails dug into the palms of his hand. "You're very kind."

He wondered that no one else heard the quiet insult behind the words. "It is our wish to make your stay here comfortable. If you will come with me." As the reporters closed in, he brushed them off. "Miss Hamilton will answer all your questions at tomorrow's press conference. Now she needs to rest after the long flight."

A few more persistent newsmen pursued them. Alexander simply took Eve's arm and drew her away.

"Your Highness, it might be best if I stay with the troupe."

"You have an assistant?"

"Yes, of course." She was forced to increase her pace to keep up with him.

"That's what assistants are for." There were muscles in the arm under the jacket, taut and sculpted. He wondered what they would feel like when they were tensed and ready to receive him. "You'd be wiser to get to the palace quickly and avoid being run over by the press."

"I can handle the press," she began, then stopped. "I'm going to the hotel. The dinner at the palace isn't for hours yet."

"You've no reason to go to the hotel." They were out the side entrance of the terminal as arranged by security and moving toward the waiting limo. "Your assistant and the members of my staff will see to the needs of your troupe."

"That's all very well and good," she began as she was forced to climb into the limo. "But I'd like to unpack myself, freshen up. I'm sure whatever we have to discuss can wait a few hours."

"Of course." He settled back and signaled to the driver.

"There's no reason for you to go out of your way to take me to the hotel when I could go with the rest."

"You aren't staying at the hotel. You stay at the palace. It's been arranged."

"Then unarrange it." The formality, as well as the brief moment of weakness, was gone. "I'm staying at the hotel with my people."

"It serves neither you nor me for you to stay at the hotel." Calmly he pushed a button. A compact bar slid out. "Would you like a drink?"

"No, I wouldn't like a drink, I'd like an explanation of why I'm being kidnapped."

He'd forgotten she could amuse him. After pouring himself a glass of mineral water, he smiled at her. "Strong words, Eve. My father would be interested that you find our invitation to the palace tantamount to kidnapping."

"This has nothing to do with your father."

"It is at his request that you stay with us. The security at the hotel has, of course, been strengthened."

"Why?"

"These are uneasy times."

There was a ripple of anxiety, but it was for him, not her, not her company. "So your sister said to me a few months ago. Your Highness, if you or your father feels there's danger, I want to be with my people."

"I understand." He set down his glass. "The hotel is very secure, Eve, and we don't feel your troupe is in any danger. My father feels, and I agree, that you, because of your personal connection with our family, are another matter. We would prefer it if you'd stay in the palace if for no other reason than to avoid the reporters who will clog the hotel lobby for the next few weeks. Or you can simply accept the invitation because my father is fond of you."

"You put it so that if I do what I choose I'm ungracious."

"Yes." He smiled again and picked up his glass.

"Very well, I accept your invitation. And I'll have some diet soda—something with caffeine. A lot of caffeine."

"You're tired from the flight."

"From the flight," she agreed as he added ice to a glass. "From the weeks before the flight. I think I've been averaging about five hours a night between preproduction meetings, auditions, dry rehearsing and paperwork. I didn't realize all my people would have to go through the security clearances." Absently she fiddled with the daisy. He watched her fingers stroke the white petals. "Then when I hired two more, we had to rush them through. I hope it's worth it." She sipped and waited for the caffeine to jolt her system back to life.

"Do you doubt it?"

"Only several times a day." Her feet had eased out of the toes of her shoes without her being conscious of it. Her shoulders were relaxed. Heavy, her eyes drooped down to sensuous slits. "I am pleased with the new people. She's an ingenue, straight out of college, with a lot of potential. I'm going to have her understudy the second lead in the Neil Simon play. And Russ Talbot's a real pro. He's done a lot of little theater and off-off-Broadway stuff. We're lucky to have him. He's cast as Brick for *Cat on a Hot Tin Roof*. That's going to be our first production."

She drank again and hoped she wasn't making a mistake there. It was such a steamy play, such a passionate one. For weeks she'd toyed with doing a comedy first, to give both the audience and the troupe a running start. Instinct had her opting for Tennessee Williams as an opener.

"I sent copies of all the scripts with the staging. I assume your assistant has read them all."

"They've been read," he said simply. By him. There was no need for her to know now just how closely he intended to work with her. "They've been approved—tentatively."

"Tentatively." That had been something that had had her back up for weeks. "I find it difficult to understand why you feel it necessary to have two alternates. From an artistic angle and a practical one, it's going to be very difficult if we have to switch things around now. We open in three weeks."

"Time enough to replace one of your productions if we find it unsuitable."

"Unsuitable? Just who makes that kind of judgment? You?"

He studied his mineral water and said nothing for a moment. There was no one, no one outside his immediate family, who would have dared use that tone with him. Deciding on patience, Alexander wondered if Americans were audacious as a rule, or if she were simply an exception.

"In my capacity as president of the center, the final judgment would be mine."

"Swell." She chugged down more soda. "Just swell. Prince or president, you don't make my life easy. I selected these four because—"

"I'll listen to your reasons tomorrow. We have a meeting scheduled for—nine, I believe. You'll meet Cornelius Manderson, who manages the center. My sister will also be there."

"I can be grateful to have at least one reasonable person around."

"Eve, you go on the defensive before it's necessary."

"Boy Scout motto."

"Pardon?"

"Be prepared," she said, and was amused enough to smile. "All right, then, I won't pick a fight yet. Tomorrow's another matter. I'm ready to go to the wall on this, Your Highness, and you're going to find I'm not easy to beat."

"I'm aware of that already." And he was already looking forward to it. "Perhaps it would be best if we agreed to keep our personal relationship separate from our work at the center."

She held her glass in her hand and tried to concentrate on the palace as they rode through the gates. It always gave her a sense of peace and security. But not this time. She shifted a bit in her seat. "We haven't got a personal relationship."

"No?"

When she turned her head she was surprised and a bit unnerved to see he was amused. She wasn't going to find his smiles as easy to deal with as his scowls. "No. What happened the last time was..." Finding no definition available, she shrugged the attempt away.

"Was unfortunate," he finished, then took her empty glass and set it down. "Unfortunate that it occurred in that manner and ended poorly. Shall I apologize?"

"No, I'd rather you didn't."

"Why?"

"Because then I'd have to accept your apology." Taking a deep breath, she faced him directly. "If I don't accept it, I'll stay annoyed with you and it won't happen again."

"There's a flaw in your logic, Eve." He continued to sit after the car stopped at the palace steps. Even when the driver opened the door, Alexander stayed where he was, watching her, compelling her to watch him. "You are most often annoyed with me, yet it did happen. But for the sake of your argument, I won't apologize."

He stepped from the car and offered his hand, leaving her no choice but to accept it. "Somehow I think I was outmaneuvered," she muttered.

"You were." Then he smiled, abruptly charming, and led her up the palace steps.

She matched her steps with his, but for the first time found herself hesitating to pass through the large ornate doors of the palace. "I never considered you much of a game player, Your Highness."

"On the contrary, I enjoy games very much."

"Chess, fencing, polo." She moved her shoulders restlessly. "Not people games."

Her scent was the same, the same as it had been the last time he'd seen her, touched her. The same scent that had awoken him in the middle of the night when she'd been thousands of miles away. "You called me a politician. What is politics but a people game?" The heavy door slid open soundlessly. Eve sent him a long, cautious look before she stepped inside.

"My father wishes to see you. I'll take you to him. Your bags should arrive shortly."

"All right." She started up the steps beside him. "The prince is well?"

"Yes." He wouldn't elaborate on her unspoken question. The Paris incident wasn't a closed book, but one he thought it best to leave untouched.

Feeling the snub, Eve started the climb from the second to the third floor in silence. "You don't want me to speak of what happened in Paris to your father."

"There's no reason for you to speak of it."

"Of course not." The words came out with the brittleness of hurt. "It was nothing to me, after all." She swung up the last of the stairs and down the hall ahead of him, only to be forced to wait at the closed door that led to Prince Armand's office.

"Your emotions remain too close to the surface," Alexander noted. He'd recognized this, even envied it, as a man who'd been forced year after year to keep his own buried. "That wasn't said to offend you."

"No, you don't have to deliberately try to offend."

"*Touché,*" he said with something close to a sigh.

"I don't want to cross swords with you. I don't expect you to include me in your family feelings." She looked away and didn't see his gaze come back to search her face. "The sad thing is you've never understood that I care very much." She folded her arms as if to distance herself when he stared at her. "Will you knock?"

He didn't. A man in his position could afford few mistakes. When he made one, it was best to admit it quickly. "He'll look strained, a bit thinner. The incident in Paris weighs on him." Alexander looked at the closed door, recognizing it for a barricade, one that someday he would have to use. "He doesn't sleep well."

"What can I do?"

God, could it be so simple for her? The words made him want to rest his brow against hers, only for a moment. Rest, be comforted, be eased. But it could never be so simple for him. "You're doing it," he said briefly, and knocked.

"Entrez."

"Father." Alexander opened the door, then stepped to the side. "I've brought you a gift."

Prince Armand rose from his desk. He was a sternly handsome man, straight and lean. When Eve had first met him, his hair had been threaded with gray. Now it was steely, like his eyes, like his body. Seeing her, he smiled, and the rigid lines softened.

"A lovely one." He came around the desk to her in a gesture of friendship she knew wasn't given to many. As she curtsied, he caught both her hands. His were strong. If age sat lightly on him, responsibility didn't. She saw the signs of strain, of sleeplessness, and forgot protocol. Rising on her toes, she kissed both his cheeks.

"It's good to be back, Your Highness."

"It's you who are good for us. Alexander, you didn't tell me she'd grown more beautiful."

"He doesn't notice," she said with a careless glance over her shoulder.

"On the contrary. I simply didn't think it necessary to explain what my father would see for himself."

"A born diplomat," Armand said, and laughed. "Alex, ring for tea, please. We'll keep Eve to ourselves for a little while before we have to share her with the rest of Cordina. So, the young girl is now an important producer." He led her to a chair. "You've come to entertain us."

"I hope so."

"My son tells me the center is fortunate to have your company. Your reputation in America is growing, and as your first international host, we're honored."

Eve smiled. "Bennett loves to flatter."

"True enough." Armand drew out a cigarette. "But in this case it was Alex."

"Alex?" Caught off guard, she turned her head to stare as Alexander took a chair beside her.

"Eve doesn't expect flattery from me, Father." He drew out his lighter and flicked it at the end of his father's cigarette. "She's more prepared to dodge a blow."

"Well, when you've been doing it for seven years, it gets to be—" She caught herself, bit her tongue smartly, then turned back to the prince. "I beg your pardon, Your Highness."

"There's no need. I'm used to squabbling children. Here's our tea. Will you pour, Eve?"

"Yes, of course."

Allowing himself the luxury of relaxing, Armand sat back as the tray was set beside Eve. "Alexander tells me you've chosen four interesting plays. The first is a rather passionate and—what is the word you used, Alex?"

"Steamy," he said, and smiled at Eve's quick look.

"Yes, a steamy story set in your American South. It deals with a family?"

"Yes, Your Highness." She handed him his tea. "A power struggle within a family, both for money and for love. A rich, dominating father, two brothers, one the black sheep, the other a weakling, and their manipulative wives. It's really a story of needs and disillusionment as much as passion."

"A story that holds true in any culture."

"I'm counting on it." She handed Alexander his tea but avoided looking at him. "The plays I've chosen all lean heavily on emotion, though the two comedies accent the lighter side. My troupe's looking forward to working here. I want to thank you for giving us the opportunity."

"It was Alex who did the work and dealt with the board of directors for the center. From some of his comments, I take it they were not as open-minded as he would have liked.''

Alexander's strong fingers curled around the delicate china handle. ''They simply needed some persuasion.''

She couldn't imagine Alexander going to bat for her. At the first flutter of pleasure, Eve pulled herself back. He'd done it for himself—more accurately, for Cordina. ''However it was arranged, I'm grateful. We won't disappoint you.''

''I'm sure you won't. I'm looking forward to meeting the rest of your company this evening.''

Understanding this to be a gentle dismissal, Eve rose. ''If you'll excuse me, then, I'd better get unpacked.'' Because her nature demanded it, she kissed Armand's cheek again. ''It really is good to be back.''

Though her bags weren't yet delivered, Eve's room was ready, scented with fresh flowers, windows open to the sea. Slipping out of her shoes, then her jacket, she pushed the billowing curtains aside.

The view took her breath away. It was the same every time—the initial disbelief that anything could be that beautiful, then the dizzying pleasure that it was real. The gardens were far below, vivid, delightful in color. Whoever had planted them, whoever tended them, appreciated the need for flowers to grow as they pleased, rather than in neat, orderly rows. The result was dreamlike rather than perfection.

Beyond the garden was the seawall, worn smooth by centuries of wind and salt. The cliff fell off sharply then, sheerly vertical with juts and mounds of rocks for seabirds to nest in. Then there was the sea itself, dark, deep, radiantly blue. Boats glided across it now.

She saw a boat with red sails racing with the wind, and a pleasure yacht so white it hurt the eyes. Someone was waterskiing. She squinted to see if it was a man or woman, but distance made the figure just a figure skimming along the

searing blue surface. Enchanted, she knelt on the window
seat, propped her chin on her hands and continued to watch.

The knock at her door meant her bags had arrived. Half
dreaming, Eve stayed where she was. *"Entrez, s'il vous
plaît."*

"It's been arranged for you to have a maid."

Alexander's voice had her jolting straight and nearly losing her balance on the window seat. "Oh, thank you, but it
really isn't necessary."

Alexander murmured to the servant to set her bags down
and leave. "She can deal with your unpacking at your con-
venience. Her name is Collette. She won't disturb you until
you ring."

"Thank you."

"You look tired." Without the jacket, she looked more
fragile, more approachable, almost as if she were a woman
he could sit with, talk with, be only a man with. He wanted
to smooth the hair from her brow, gently, even tenderly. His
hands curled at his sides. "You might want to rest first."

"No, I'm not tired really. I've just been hypnotizing myself with the view."

She waited for him to leave, but instead he crossed to her,
drawing the curtains aside a little more. "I have the same
view from my window."

"I suppose you're used to it, then. I don't think I'd ever
be."

"Early, just after dawn, the fishing boats go out." He
rested his hand on the sill beside hers. Eve's gaze was drawn
to it, to the long, tanned fingers, the wide back and the ring
that stated who and what he was. "They look so fragile, yet
they go out day after day."

His hands fascinated her. They had touched her once, not
gently but potently. There was strength in them a woman
could rely on, as well as a strength to be feared. She wondered why at the moment she should feel only the first.

"I've never been a terribly good sailor myself, but I like
to watch. When I was young, my father had a sailboat. I was

forever tangling up the lines or getting bashed by the boom. Eventually he got tired of it and bought a powerboat. I had a shot at waterskiing.''

"Did you have better luck?" he asked.

"Some." She turned again and searched for the sexless skier. As she did, he or she took an impressive spill. Laughing, Eve leaned back on her heels. "That was about as good as I got, too."

"So you prefer to swim."

"I prefer to have control. That's why I took up karate. I like making my own moves rather than being at the mercy of the wind or a towline or whatever."

"Not at the mercy of the wind," Alexander corrected. "You work with or outwit the wind."

"Maybe you do."

"I could teach you."

Surprised—no, stunned—she looked up at him. It had been said casually, but she'd never known him to do anything casually. She could imagine herself sailing with him, the sun, the wind, his body gleaming in the shimmering light. She could imagine it too well. "Thank you, but my father already judged me hopeless."

"You were a child." The breeze ruffled her hair against his arm. "You're not a child now."

"No." Unnerved and feeling foolish because of it, she looked out the window again. "But I doubt either of us will have much time for sailing lessons while I'm here. Work starts tomorrow."

"And today?"

Her heart was pounding in her throat. It was ridiculous. She wasn't subject to flights of fancy and wide swings of emotion. Meet it head on, Eve advised herself. Meet it head on and push it aside. She turned again and looked at him. "I don't know what you want. I don't—" When he reached down to brush the hair from her cheek, the words simply slid away.

"I think you do."

"No." She managed to find the strength to shake her head. "That's impossible."

"So I've told myself." His fingers tightened on her hair. His eyes weren't so secretive now. In them she saw need, and felt the longing grow in herself to fulfill it. "It becomes more difficult to accept."

"Your Highness." Her hand flew to his wrist when he framed her face. "Alex, please, this isn't right."

"The hell with right."

He took her then, mouth, soul and heart, as the salt-scented breeze billowed at the curtains. Her hands were still at his wrists, her fingers clamping harder and harder, whether in denial or acceptance neither of them knew.

He'd wanted, needed, yearned for the passion and spirit that were so much a part of her. He'd craved the softness and sweetness that offset the rest. If it was wrong, if it was impossible, he'd fight his way through the obstacles. He'd known, the moment he'd seen her again, that he had no choice.

How could she deny what was happening to her? She wasn't a woman who lied to herself, who refused to see her own flaws. Desire, hot and liquid, ruled her thoughts. And it was Alexander, heir to the throne, whom she wanted. Desperately, she realized. Uncontrollably. Even as she tried to reason it out, her body was pulsing with more needs.

To be his, she thought as she released his wrist to comb her fingers through his hair. To be his would be everything.

He was edging toward madness. She was so smooth, so warm. The fire was licking at him, what was his, what had come from her. If he didn't bank it now, it would overwhelm both of them. He couldn't allow it to happen this way, not now, not here. Alexander drew her away, swore, then kissed her again until she went limp in his arms.

"You'll have to choose." His voice wasn't steady, but he drew her head back and kept his eyes on hers. "And you'll have to choose soon."

She ran a hand that trembled over her face. "I don't understand."

"I don't intend to lose." He had her hair in his hand, holding her still. She wouldn't have moved in any case. His eyes would have held her. "Understand that. I didn't apologize for before, and I won't apologize now."

He released her, then strode to the door and out.

Alone, Eve eased herself down on the seat like a woman who'd had too much sun or wine. Perhaps she'd had both somehow. His kiss had been both hot and potent. She had to think. With a shaky sigh, she pressed her fingers to her eyes. The trouble was, she didn't know where to start.

Chapter Five

Eve felt secure in the theater, satisfied with the office that had been prepared for her and grateful for the hours per day she would have away from the palace. And Alexander.

She was a professional woman. A businesswoman with her career in full swing and the ultimate success just at the tip of her fingers. Her biggest challenge to date was spread out before her. Nearly a hundred people were depending on her to make decisions, give orders and do things right. She couldn't afford to spend her nights tossing and turning, trying to figure out a man. She couldn't daydream about him when there were a million things to be done.

But when he'd kissed her in front of the window with the scent of the sea creeping in around them, it had been no less devastating, no less illuminating than the first time. Need, both sharply physical and deeply emotional, had run through her. Not need for a man, for a lover, for a companion, but for Alexander. She'd wanted him—to make love with her there near the window while the sky and the sea were still a perfect blue.

It wouldn't have been lovemaking, Eve reminded herself as she pressed fingers against her tired eyes. It would have been sex, plain and simple. She didn't want that, didn't need it, and she wasn't going to think of it anymore.

It was barely two on her first full day in Cordina. Her morning meeting had gone well enough. Alexander had been more his familiar self—distant, businesslike and exacting. That was a man she knew how to deal with. The man who had kissed her the afternoon before, the man who had made her feel weak and strong and desperate all at once—she didn't know how to deal with him.

He'd been the perfect host to her company the evening before. His charm was on the formal side, but her people had been impressed. In fact, she mused, more than one of her female players had been overly impressed. She'd have to keep her eyes open. It wouldn't do to have anyone distracted over the next few weeks. Including her. With that in mind she began checking and cross-checking her lists.

The glamour of theater, she thought wryly as she rubbed the back of her neck. Just how many tubes of makeup had they shipped—and where the hell were they? Then there was the crate of cable that had left Houston just fine, but had never made the transfer in New York. If the airport didn't call her back by four, she was going to—

"Yes, come in." Harried, Eve barely glanced up. "Yes, Russ. There can't be a problem already can there? But wait." She held up a hand before he could speak. "You and the rest of the troupe aren't due in until tomorrow, right?"

"Yes to both questions. There is a problem already and I'm not due in—but I couldn't stay away." He was a young-looking thirty with a well-built body and a lantern jaw. Eve had liked his looks from the beginning, but had still put him through three readings before she'd signed him. The wavy blond hair and the blue eyes were a plus, but she looked for substance. She'd never have cast him as Brick if she hadn't found it. When he perched on the edge of her desk, she leaned back and grimaced.

"Tell me the problem first."

"Lighting director's having an artistic difference with a twenty K spotlight. Nobody can put his hands on the crate of extra bulbs."

"I'm surprised anyone can put his hands on anything now. Okay, I'll see to it in a minute. Tell me why you're not out soaking up the sun while you have the chance?" She smiled and tucked a pencil behind her ear. "Hasn't anyone warned you what a slave driver I am? You show up at the theater, you go to work."

"That's what I'm counting on." His voice was deep and resonant. Still, she wanted him to practice the lazy drawl of his character until it was second nature. "Look, I don't want to sound green, but this place . . ." He lifted his palms a bit dramatically and took in more than her office. "It's amazing. Being here's amazing. I can soak up sun anytime. If I can't rehearse, I can unpack crates."

"You don't sound green, you sound psychotic." With a laugh, she stood. "And I know just what you mean. Crates, it is. God knows we've got plenty of them. Now why don't we—"

Her door swung open again, this time without a knock. Bennett grinned at her. "They told me I'd find you locked in here and snarling."

"I'm not snarling. Yet." She got up immediately and opened her arms for a hug. "Prince Bennett, Russ Talbot."

Russ hesitated between offering a hand, bowing or standing still. "I'm never sure how to greet princes."

"We say hello," Bennett told him. "I hated missing the dinner last night and meeting your troupe."

"What you missed was seeing how many pretty actresses you could flirt with." Eve picked up her clipboard.

"There's that." He shot his grin at Russ. "Are there many?"

"Enough."

"I knew I could count on Eve. In any case, I've come to take you away from all this."

"Fine." She looked up from her notations. "Come back in two hours."

"Two hours?"

"Better make it three," she corrected after a glance at her clipboard.

"Eve, you'll wear yourself out."

"Wear myself out?" Laughing, she nudged him out into the hall with her. "I haven't even started yet. I could use the lift, though, if it's not putting you out. Say—" She looked at her watch "—five-thirty?"

"All right if—"

"Unless you'd like to stay. We're about to uncrate boxes."

"I'll be back." He gave her a quick kiss before he started down the corridor. "Nice meeting you, Talbot."

"That's the first time I've ever seen royalty get the bum's rush."

Eve sent Russ a smile. "Much as I love him, he'd be in the way."

"Not much like his brother," Russ commented.

"Ben?" Eve shook her head as they walked in the opposite direction. "No. No, he's not."

"Gets a lot of press."

She couldn't prevent the chuckle. "Bennett would tell you it's all true."

"Is it?"

She glanced at him. Her voice cooled a bit. "Possibly."

"Sorry." Russ dipped his hands into his pockets. "I didn't mean to pry. It's just—well, it's interesting, and I'm as susceptible as anyone. It's weird you being so tight with them. We didn't have many royal highnesses in Montclair."

"They're just people." She stopped at the door to one of the storerooms. "No, of course they're not. But they are people, and nice ones. You'll see that for yourself in the next few weeks."

Then she opened the door, stepped back and moaned. Russ peered in around her shoulder at the stacks of trunks and crates. "Looks like we could use some help."

"You go call out the marines," Eve told him, and pushed up her sleeves. "I'll get started."

Within three hours Eve had the beginnings of order and a long list of things to be done. With the help of Russ and a couple of stagehands, the crates were uncarted or stacked for storage until their contents were needed. She worked methodically, as was her style, and lifted and grunted as much as the men who worked with her. After twenty minutes, Russ had stopped telling her not to lift that, not to shove this. She was, he'd discovered, as strong as the rest of them.

By five she was sweaty, smudged and ruffled, but far from displeased.

"Russ, go home." She leaned against one of the crates and wished fleetingly for something long and cool.

"What about you?"

"I've nearly done all I can for the moment, and I don't want my actors too exhausted to rehearse." She wiped her forehead with the back of her hand. "You've been a big help. The rest of this is really up to me and the crew."

He dried the sweat on his face with a sleeve before giving her a look of amused admiration. "I don't know many producers who get their hands dirty."

Eve turned her palms up and wrinkled her nose at the smears of dust. "Apparently this producer does. Ten o'clock call tomorrow. Be fresh."

"Yes, ma'am. Any messages for the rest of the troupe?"

"The same. Tell them to enjoy the evening, but any hangovers tomorrow morning won't be sympathized with."

"I'll keep that in mind. Don't work too hard."

She glanced around as he left the storeroom. "Tell me about it." Hands on hips, she decided she'd done about all the damage she could do for one day. Putting her back into it, she scooted one last box of bulbs into a corner. At the sound behind her, she dug into the pockets of her sweats and pulled out a set of keys.

"Give these to Gary, will you? He'll need to get in here first thing tomorrow." Without looking, she chucked the keys.

"I'd be happy to oblige if I knew who Gary was and where to find him."

"Oh." Still stooped, she looked up at Alex. His light sweater and slacks were spotless, his hair unruffled and his shoes shined. She felt like a dustrag. "I thought you were one of the stagehands."

"No." When she straightened, he tossed the keys back to her. "Eve, have you been in here shoving at these crates?"

"I've been unpacking and, uh..." She linked her filthy hands behind her back. "Organizing."

"And moving things entirely too heavy to be moved by a woman."

"Now just a minute—"

"Let's say too heavy to be moved by someone of your size and build."

The rephrasing mollified only because her back ached. "I had help."

"Apparently not enough. If you need more, you've only to ask."

"We can manage, thanks. The worst of it's done." She attempted to clean off her hands on the front of her sweats. "I didn't realize you were coming in today. Was there something we left out this morning?"

He came farther into the room. She stood with her hands behind her back and her back against a crate. "We have no business to discuss."

"Well, then." She caught herself moistening her lips. "I'd better get these keys to Gary and clean up before Bennett gets here." She started forward, but he stood in her way.

"Bennett was detained. I've come to take you home."

"That wasn't necessary." She moved to the side as he stepped forward. "I told Ben I'd take the lift if it was convenient." He moved again, and she evaded. "I don't expect to be driven around while I'm here. Renting a car's simple enough."

She smelled like hot honey baked in the sun and waiting to be sampled. "Do you object to driving with me?"

"No, of course not." She rapped her heel on a crate, then stood her ground. "You're stalking me."

"It would seem so." He ran a fingertip down her cheek, and was pleased to detect the slightest tremor. "You're filthy."

"Yes. I do have to clean up, so if you don't want to wait, I can catch a ride with— A cab. I can take a cab."

"I can wait. It's amazing that you manage to be beautiful even under all that dirt. Beautiful." He rubbed his thumb over her lips. "Desirable."

"Alex. Alexander. I don't know why you're... It's difficult to understand why..."

His hand curled loosely around her neck.

"I wish you wouldn't."

"Wouldn't what?"

"Try to seduce me."

"I don't intend merely to try."

"This is ridiculous." But when she tried to shift away, he blocked her again. "You don't even like me, really, and I—well I've always..." His eyes were so dark, dark, amused and as hypnotic as the view from her window. "That is, I've always thought that..."

"I don't recall that you stuttered before."

"I didn't. I don't." She passed a hand through her hair. "You're making me very nervous."

"I know. It's amazingly rewarding."

"Well, I don't like it. No," she said weakly, when he lowered his mouth to hers. This time it wasn't wild or desperate, but soft and teasing. The hand she had lifted in protest fell limply to her side. She didn't reach for him, didn't touch him, but stood swaying... floating... drowning.

The triumph should have moved through him. She was his now; he could feel it in the way her head fell back, her lips parted. At that moment she was completely open to him, his to fill with whatever needs moved through him. But instead of triumph came an ache, a need to stroke, protect, soothe. Promise. He wanted the thrill, and was left with the thirst.

"Go wash your face," he murmured, and stepped aside.

Eve was out of the room faster than dignity allowed.

* * *

Eve took a hard look at herself in the mirror of the rest room backstage. She was making a fool of herself—and it was going to stop. For whatever reason of his own, Alexander had decided to play games. That didn't mean she had to go along with it. He was making her feel foolish. Look foolish. She could tolerate a great deal, but not that. Pride was vital to her, pride in who she was, in what she'd made of and for herself. She wasn't going to turn into a babbling idiot because Alexander had suddenly decided she'd make a good playmate. Or bedmate.

That made her swallow quickly. Years before she'd hoped for his attention, even in her girlish way dreamed of it. She'd been stung by his disinterest, galled by his silent disapproval. She'd gotten over all of that. She scrubbed at her hands for the third time.

Maybe the problem was that she'd begun to think of Alexander as a person again, as a man. Things would be better if she thought of him as His Royal Highness—a title, aloof, lofty and a bit cold,

It didn't come easy when she could still feel the way the warmth had transferred from his lips to hers.

Why was he doing this? Eve stuffed her brush back into her bag. It was so totally out of character. For both of them, she realized. If she had written a play with Alexander as the lead, she would never have staged a scene like the one that had just occurred. No one would believe it.

So why didn't she ask him? Before she could laugh the idea off, it began to make sense. She was a blunt, no-nonsense woman; Alexander was a cautious diplomat. She'd put the question to him flat out, then watch him dangle for words. Pleased with the plan, she swung back into the corridor.

"An improvement," Alexander said easily, and took her arm before she could evade it.

"Thank you. I think we should talk."

"Good idea." He pushed the stage door open and led her outside. "We can take a drive before we go home."

"It's not necessary. It won't take long."

"I'm sure it's more than necessary for you to have some fresh air after being cooped up all day." When he opened the door of the steel-gray Mercedes, Eve stopped.

"What's this?"

"My car."

"But there's no driver."

"Would you like to see my license?" When she continued to hesitate, he smiled. "Eve, you're not afraid of being alone with me, are you?"

"Of course not." She tried to sound indignant, but looked restlessly over her shoulder. Two bodyguards, blank faced and burly, stood at the car behind them. "Besides, you're never really alone."

Alexander followed the direction of her gaze. The quick sensation of restraint didn't reach his eyes. "Unfortunately some things other than fresh air are necessary."

What he felt didn't reach his eyes, didn't show on his face, but she thought she caught a trace of it in his voice. "You hate it."

He glanced back, surprised and more than a little wary that she'd seen what he so carefully tried to hide. "It's a waste of time to hate the necessary." Alexander gestured her into the car, shut the door behind her and rounded the hood. He didn't glance at or acknowledge the guards. "Your seat belt," he murmured as he started the engine.

"What? Oh." Eve stopped rehearsing her speech and pulled the harness into place. "I've always enjoyed driving around Cordina," she began. Be friendly, she advised herself. Be casual, then zero in when he least expects it. "It's such a lovely city. No skyscrapers, no steel-and-glass boxes."

"We continue to fight certain kinds of progress." He eased into the light traffic. "Several times hotel chains have lobbied to build resorts. The advantages are there, of course, an increase in employment, tourism.''

''No.'' She shook her head as she studied the town. ''It could never be worth it.''

''This from the daughter of a builder?''

''What Daddy's built and where he's built it has generally been a good thing. Houston's . . . Houston's different. A city like that needs to be developed.''

''There are some on the council who would argue that Cordina needs to be developed.''

''They're wrong.'' She turned to him. ''Obviously your father feels the same way. What about you? When your turn comes, will you let them dig into the rock?''

''No.'' He turned away from the city and toward the sea. ''Some things are meant to grow naturally. The palace is the highest building in the country. As long as a Bisset lives there, it will remain so.''

''Is that ego?''

''That is heritage.''

And she could accept it. ''We're so different,'' she said, half to herself. ''You speak of heritage and you mean centuries of responsibility and tradition. When I think of it, I think of my father's business and the headache someone's going to be saddled with one day. Or I think of my mother's Fabergé bowl. Heritage for me, and I suppose for most Americans, is tangible. You can hold it in your hand. For you it's more nebulous, but a hundred times more binding.''

For several moments he said nothing. She couldn't know how deeply her words, her empathy had affected him. ''You understand better than I expected.''

She glanced at him quickly, then as quickly away. She couldn't be moved. She didn't dare allow it. ''Why are you doing this?''

''Doing what?''

''Driving me along the beach, coming to the theater? Why did you kiss me that way?''

"Which way?"

She might have laughed if she hadn't felt so adrift. "Any way. Why did you kiss me at all?"

He considered as he looked for a private spot by the sea-wall. "The most obvious answer is that I wanted to."

"That's not obvious at all. You never wanted to before."

"Women aren't as perceptive as they would like the world to think." He stopped the car, shut off the engine and slipped the keys into his pocket. "I've wanted to since the first time I saw you. Would you like to walk?"

While she sat stunned, he got out and came around to her door.

"You have to unhook your seat belt."

"That's not true."

"I'm afraid it's difficult to walk on the beach if you're strapped to a car seat."

Eve fumbled with the lock, then sprang out of the car. "I meant what you just said wasn't true. You hardly even looked at me, and when you did it was to scowl."

"I looked at you a great deal." He took her hand and began to walk toward the sand. Her fingers were stiff in his, resisting. He ignored the feeling. It was easier for him when she held herself back, challenged him to outmaneuver. Her one moment of absolute surrender had terrified him. "I prefer the beach in the evening, when the tourists have gone in to change for dinner."

"That's absurd."

His smile was friendly, and sweeter than she could ever remember seeing it. "It's absurd to prefer a quiet beach?"

"I wish you'd stop twisting things around that way." Eve shook her hand free and stepped back a few paces. "I don't know what kind of game you're playing."

"What kind would you like?" He stood where he was, pleased, even relieved to see her confusion. It made it easier somehow to get closer without taking a step.

"Alexander, you did not spend a great deal of time looking at me. I know because—" She cut herself off, appalled that she'd been about to admit how she'd mooned over him.

"Because?"

"I just know, that's all." She brushed the subject away with the back of her hand and started toward the water. "I don't understand why you've suddenly decided you find me attractive or available or whatever."

"Finding you attractive is not sudden." He put a hand on her shoulder and with the slightest of pressure made her turn. The sun would be setting soon. She could see it behind him, spreading golden light. The sand beneath her feet was white and cool, but she discovered as she stared up at him that it was far from solid. "Whether you are available or not no longer matters. I want you." He paused, letting his hand slide over her shoulder to her nape. "I find that matters a great deal more."

She shuddered and crossed her arms over her chest. Her eyes were as blue as the sea now, but more, much more turbulent. "And because you're a prince you can have whatever you want."

The breeze over the sea blew her hair around his fingers. He forgot the beach, the guards, the sun that had yet to set. "Because I'm a prince it's more difficult for me to have what I want. Particularly when what I want is a woman."

"An American woman." Her breath came quickly, erratically. It would have been so easy not to question, but to accept. She wanted to accept, to move into his arms, maybe into his heart. Discovering that was what she wanted most changed everything and compounded the questions. "An American woman who makes her living in the theater. No rank, no pedigree. Not as suitable for an affair as another aristocrat, another European."

"No." He said it simply and watched the hurt come into her eyes. But he wouldn't lie. "To have my name linked with yours wouldn't be suitable to certain members of the council, certain high officials. It's more agreeable when I socialize with a woman of title or with an ancestry.''

"I see." She brought her hand up and removed his from her neck. "So it would be more ... tactful if I agreed to a clandestine affair.''

Anger transformed his face into hard, unyielding lines. No one seeing him now would believe he could smile so sweetly. "I don't believe I asked you to be tactful.''

"No, you hadn't gotten to it yet." She was going to cry. The knowledge stunned her, humiliated her. Humiliation snapped her back straight and kept her eyes dry—so dry they hurt. "Well, thanks for the offer, Your Highness, but I'm not interested. When I sleep with a man, I do so with no shame. When I have a relationship with a man, it's in the open.''

"I'm aware of that.''

She'd started to storm away, but his words brought her up short. "Just what do you mean?''

"You've been very open about your relationship with my brother." There was no smile now, or any sign of temper. His eyes were flat and dark. "Apparently you've had no shame there, either.''

Confusion came first, then a glimmer, then a flash of insight. Because it was safer than being hurt, Eve let her fury take her. "So that's what this is all about. Some sibling rivalry, some curiosity about your brother's taste. What did you think, Alex, he'd had his turn, now you wanted to see what all the fuss was about?''

He stood where he was, knowing he didn't dare step toward her. "Be careful.''

She was beyond care, but not yet beyond words. "The hell with you. You may be an aristocrat, a prince, a ruler, but underneath you're as much a fool as any other man and I won't stand here and explain or justify my relationship with Bennett to a fool. You could take lessons from him, Alex. He has a heart and a genuine affection for women. He doesn't consider them trophies to be passed around.''

"Are you finished?"

"Oh, more than. I suggest you speak to Bennett, Your Highness, if you want to find out my . . . pros and cons. I'm sure you'd be fascinated."

"What I was feeling for you had nothing to do with Bennett—and everything to do with him. I'll drive you back."

He started toward the car. The two guards who'd kept at a discreet distance climbed into theirs.

Chapter Six

"Ethel, I want another white slip for *Cat*." Clipboard in hand, Eve was going through the costumes, one item at a time, with her wardrobe mistress.

"White slip. Size thirty-four."

"Not too low cut. I want some subtlety."

"A subtle white slip. Size thirty-four."

Eve chuckled, but continued to go through the wardrobe for the first production. "Let's keep within budget. Make it nylon—as long as it looks like silk."

"She wants a miracle."

"Always. Oh, and let out Big Daddy's jackets, say, an inch and a half. I'm going to want Jared padded a bit more."

Ethel chewed her stick of peppermint gum while she noted down instructions. She'd been in wardrobe for twenty-two years. She could, with forty-five minutes notice, make a silk purse out of a sow's ear. "If the cast keeps eating the way they did the other night, you won't need any padding."

"I intend to keep an eye on that, too."

"Never doubted it." Ethel brought her half glasses down farther on her nose and looked at Eve over the straight edge. "Somebody ought to be keeping an eye on you. You give up sleeping?"

"Looks that way." She fingered two children's costumes. "These may have to be altered. I audition kids tomorrow. Let's pray we can find two who can play nasty little monsters."

"I have a couple I'm willing to lend out." Gabriella stepped into the wardrobe room.

"Brie, I was hoping you'd make it by." Tucking the clipboard under one arm, Eve embraced her with the other.

"I'd have made it by yesterday, but I had four dentist appointments, two haircuts and a meeting with an impossibly tight-pursed budget committee."

"Just another day of glamour and leisure. Princess Gabriella, may I present Miss Ethel Cohen, my miracle worker with needle and thread."

Ethel dropped into an awkward curtsy. "Your Majesty."

"We settle for 'Your Highness' in Cordina." Smiling, Gabriella offered a hand. "So many costumes." She studied the rack, the trays and boxes full of accessories, then fingered a rope of glass beads until she felt Ethel was more at ease. "How in the world do you keep track of everything?"

"I have a system, Your Highness. As long as I can keep certain people from fouling it up." She cast a narrow-eyed look at Eve.

"I'm just checking off," Eve muttered. "I'm not touching anything."

"So far," Ethel said under her breath.

"Did I hear you say that someone should keep an eye on Eve?"

"Yes, ma'am, Your Highness. Too keyed up and not sleeping right. I'd be obliged to anyone who could get her out of my hair for a while."

"A fat lot of respect the producer gets around here."

"Concern's often more important," Gabriella commented. "I believe I can help you out, Miss Cohen. I have twenty free minutes. Eve, I'd love a cup of coffee."

"Brie, I'm up to my ears—"

"I could pull rank."

Eve let out a windy sigh. "And would, too. All right, but we're going to have to make it fifteen, and in my office."

"Fair enough." Brie linked arms with Eve, then looked over her shoulder, mouthing the word twenty to Ethel.

"And how is it you have twenty free minutes in the middle of the day?"

"Luck. Nanny's with the children at the farm, Reeve's in conference with Papa and Alex, and my afternoon appointment came down with a virus."

"You don't sound sympathetic."

"I'm relieved. You have no idea how tedious it is to sit around eating watercress sandwiches—nasty things—and planning a fund-raiser with a woman with more hot air than imagination. If I'm really lucky, the virus will last three or four days and I can have the whole thing planned without her."

"Talk about nasty. Well, here, as we say in the States, is where the buck stops." She opened the door to her office and gestured Gabriella inside.

"Adequate enough," Gabriella decided, turning a circle. "But you need some fresh flowers and something to replace that hideous painting."

"I don't even notice really. It's more important that I've been requisitioned a coffee maker." Eve hit the switch. "It'll be hot in a minute."

Gabriella set her purse on the desk and casually moved to the window. "A pity you don't have a better view."

"I didn't think there was a bad view in Cordina."

Gabriella let the curtain fall back into place, then turned. "You know, Eve, I stopped by home when I dropped Reeve off. Alexander looks every bit as hollow eyed as you."

Eve moved away to busy herself with cups and saucers. "I suppose he has a lot on his mind."

"No doubt about that, and a bit more than state affairs. Did you quarrel?"

"We had words. Do you want it black or with some of this awful powdered milk?"

"Black." Gabriella waited until Eve poured and handed her a cup. "Like to talk about it?"

"He's your brother."

"And you're my friend." Without tasting, Gabriella sat and set the cup on the edge of the desk. "I love both of you, enough, I think, to be objective. Has he been difficult?"

"No." Eve took a long drink. "Impossible."

"Sounds like Alex." She couldn't prevent the hint of a smile. "In his defense I have to say he doesn't try to be impossible, he just is. What did he do?"

Eve finished off her coffee, then rose immediately to pour more. "He kissed me."

Gabriella lifted a brow, pursed her lips and considered. "That doesn't seem like such a terrible thing to me."

"Come on, Brie, I'm talking about Alexander the Proper. And he didn't just kiss me," she added because it sounded so foolish out loud. "He tried to seduce me."

"I can't believe it's taken him so long." At Eve's expression, Gabriella lifted a hand in a negligent wave. "After all, Eve, Alex may be an idiot, but he's far from stupid. It's difficult for me to believe you were shocked."

"I was shocked." Then with a grimace Eve relented. "All right, maybe I wasn't shocked, but I was surprised."

"Did you kiss him back?"

If the "him" had been anyone else, she would have laughed. "Really, Brie, that's hardly the point."

"No, it is the point, but it's also none of my business."

"I didn't mean that."

"If you didn't, you should have," Gabriella told her as she sampled her coffee. "Still, if you're angry with Alex, I think there's more to it than a kiss."

She tried to sit, then stood again to roam the room. Nothing seemed right, she thought. Nothing fit into place. "He only kissed me because of Bennett."

While Eve paced the room, Gabriella set her coffee down again. "I hate being dense, but what does Bennett have to do with Alex and you?"

"Just like a man," Eve muttered as she walked back and forth. Her oversized shirt flapped at the hips with each movement. She'd told herself she wasn't going to give it another thought. She'd promised herself that if she did think of it, she wouldn't be upset. So much for promises. She gestured with her cup and nearly sloshed coffee over the sides. "Like a little boy wanting a shiny red ball because it belongs to another little boy. Well, I'm not a red ball." She slammed her cup into its saucer. "I don't belong to anyone."

Gabriella let the silence hang a moment, then slowly nodded. "I think I'm following you. Stop me if I'm wrong. You think Alex tried to seduce you because he thinks Bennett already has."

"Bingo."

"Eve, that's absurd."

"You bet it is. I said the same thing in more graphic terms to Alexander."

"No, no, no." More than a little amused, Gabriella laughed off Eve's indignant agreement. "I meant it's absurd to think that Alex and Ben have ever played one-upmanship over anything. It simply isn't in their natures."

It wasn't the sympathy she'd counted on. Families stick together, she reminded herself, but Gabriella was a woman. She wanted a woman's reaction. "How do you explain the fact that he said I'd slept with Ben?"

"Alex said that?"

"Yes, he said it. Do you think I imagined it?"

Amusement became a shadow of concern. "No, of course not. I thought you'd misunderstood something he did or said." The concern hovered a moment, then faded. "I still do."

"It was very plain, Brie. Alex thinks Ben and I..." She left the obvious unstated as she thought it through. "Maybe everyone does."

"Anyone who sees you and Bennett together and knows you understands it's nothing but affection and friendship." She stopped, and her lips twitched a little. "Anyone who's seeing clearly."

"You'll forgive me if I don't find this as amusing as you seem to."

"I can't help but be pleased Alexander is involved with someone I respect and care for."

"We're not involved."

"Hmmm."

"Don't say hmmm—you remind me of Chris."

"Good, that means you'll think of me as a sister and listen to some advice."

It was Eve's turn to be amused. "Chris would be the first to tell you I rarely do."

"Then make an exception. Eve, I know how it is to have feelings for someone who seems totally wrong for you."

"I never said I had feelings," she said slowly. "But suppose, for the sake of argument, I did. Alexander *is* totally wrong for me. Moreover, I'm wrong for him. I have a career, one that's important to me. I have ties to another country. I like to do things when and how I choose to without deliberating how it might look to the press. I've never dealt well with rules, which I proved by doing miserably in school. Alexander lives by rules. He has to."

"True." Gabriella nodded as she sipped her coffee. "You know, Eve, your arguments are perfectly valid."

"They are?" There was a little sinking sensation in her stomach. She braced against it and spoke more firmly. "Yes, they are."

"I said I understood and I do. With the man I had feelings for, the arguments were almost identical and just as valid."

Eve poured more coffee. It seemed as though she were living on caffeine, she thought. "What did you do?"

"I married him."

Eve fought back a smile and plopped on the edge of her desk. "Thanks a lot."

Gabriella set her coffee aside, noting that Eve had drunk three to her one. And coffee, she thought, wasn't going to soothe her friend's nerves. Love made wrecks of people no matter how strong they professed to be. It hadn't been so long ago that she'd been in the turmoil of needing to love and being afraid to.

"Do you love, Alex?"

Love. The most potent four-letter word. Denying it would be easy. Honesty took more of an effort. Eve felt Gabriella deserved the truth. "I haven't let myself think of it."

"Thinking has little to do with loving. But I'm not going to pressure you any more."

Affection coursed through her as she leaned over to touch Gabriella's hand. "Brie, you could never pressure me."

"Yes, I could," Gabriella said briskly. "And it's tempting. Instead I'll tell you to try to remember that Alex has had to work very hard to develop an armor to contain his emotions. A strong, objective ruler is necessary for the country. It isn't always easy for him, or for the people close to him."

"Brie, the bottom line isn't my feelings for Alex."

"For those of us who can choose their own destinies feelings are always the bottom line."

"I wish it were so simple." If it were, she could open the door, even for a moment, and examine her own feelings, her own wants, face to face. She didn't dare. They might be much bigger and much stronger than she was. It was a matter of self-protection, she told herself. Of self-reliance. She didn't want to think it was a matter of survival.

"Brie, as much as I care for your family, I can't afford to get emotionally involved with someone who has to put country and duty ahead of me. That sounds selfish, but—"

"No, it sounds human."

"I appreciate that. You know, if—" She broke off as the phone on her desk rang. "No, don't go," she said as Gabriella started to rise. "Wait just a minute. Hello."

"Eve Hamilton?"

"Yes."

"You're close to the royal family. If you have concern for their welfare, tell them to heed a warning." The voice chilled her as much as the words. It was mechanical, sexless.

"Who is this?"

"A seeker of justice. A warning. There will be only one. François Deboque will be released from prison within forty-eight hours or a member of the royal house of Cordina will die."

With the breath backed up in her lungs, Eve shot Gabriella a look. Her friends, her family. The threat wasn't against some faceless title, but against people she loved. She gripped the phone tighter and forced aside terror. "Only a coward delivers threats anonymously."

"A warning," the voice corrected. "And a promise. Forty-eight hours."

The quiet click echoed over and over in Eve's head even after she deliberately replaced the receiver.

Fear. Because she sensed it, Gabriella rose to put a hand on Eve's. "What is it?"

When she focused on Gabriella again, Eve saw the tautness despite the Princess's attempt at composure. Taking her cue from that, she rose quickly. "Where are your bodyguards?"

"In the hall."

"Your car's outside?"

"Yes."

"A driver?"

"No, I drove myself."

"We need to go to the palace. I think one of your guards should ride with us. I'll explain on the way."

Inside Prince Armand's office, three men sat in tense conversation. Smoke hung in the room, its scent competing with that of fresh flowers and old leather. Often rooms take their mood from the man who occupies it. This one held power, quietly, unarguably. Decisions made here were rarely made in haste and never made with emotion. Decisions made here could not be regretted after the heat of anger or the twists of grief had passed.

Prince Armand sat behind his desk and listened to his son-in-law. Reeve MacGee was a man he respected and trusted. He was friend, he was family, and more, Reeve's background in law enforcement and special services made him invaluable as an adviser. Though he had refused any offer of title or position of state, Reeve had agreed to work, quietly, in the capacity of security adviser for the royal family.

"There's little more you can do to improve the security here at the palace without making a public statement."

"I have no desire to make a public statement." Armand passed a smooth white rock from hand to hand as he spoke. "The embassy?"

"The security's been upgraded there, of course. But it's my feeling that unless you're in Paris, they'll be no trouble there."

Armand accepted this with a slight inclination of his head. He knew he had been the target in Paris, and was still living, always would, with the knowledge that another man had died in his place. "And?"

Reeve needed nothing else to know the prince spoke of Deboque. "The security at the prison is excellent. However, no amount of security can prevent Deboque from issuing orders. His mail can be censored, naturally, but he's much too sharp to put anything incriminating in writing. He has a right to visitors."

"Then we agree that the Paris incident and the smaller, less tragic incidents of the past few years are Deboque's doing."

"He planted the bomb, just as he orchestrated the theft of the Lorimar diamonds from the museum two years ago. He's still running drugs while he sits in his cell. In three years, two if he manages parole, he'll be back on the streets."

Such was justice. Such was the law. "Unless we prove that through his orders, Seward was killed."

"That's right. And proof won't come easily."

"We sit here and talk about increased security. Defensive measures only." Alexander crushed his cigarette into a mass of paper and tobacco, but his voice was calm. "Where is our offense?"

Armand held the white rock a moment longer, then set it on the desk. He understood Alexander better than anyone, the tightly controlled fury, the constantly blocked emotions. A father can feel regret even as he feels pride. "You have a suggestion?"

"The longer we sit and do nothing but defend, the longer he has to plan. He has a right to visitors under the law. We know that whoever comes to Deboque is tied to Deboque." Each time he said the name it left a bitter taste on his tongue. "I'm sure Reeve can give us a report on each and every visitor in the past seven years." He glanced at his brother-in-law and received a nod. "We know who they are, what they are and where they are. Isn't it time we used that knowledge more forcibly?"

"They are under surveillance," Armand reminded him.

"Surveillance on known members of Deboque's organization did nothing for Seward." The pain was still raw and still meticulously controlled by both father and son. Silence hung a moment, broken only by the click and flare of Reeve's lighter. "We need someone on the inside."

"Alexander is right." Reeve blew out a stream of smoke. "It's something I've been giving a lot of thought to. The problem would be finding the right operative, then getting him in. Infiltrating Deboque's organization could take months."

"It took him little time to plant his woman as Gabriella's secretary." Alexander's resentment hadn't faded after seven years, only evolved into a simmering need for retribution.

Reeve understood, acknowledged, then shook his head. "It's easier to fake a security clearance, a background, records, than it is to gain a position of trust with a man like Deboque. He's in jail now only through five years of Interpol's concentrated effort."

"And still he pulls strings," Armand murmured.

"And still he pulls strings." Reeve picked up his cooling coffee only to wash the taste of frustration from his mouth. "Even after we've succeeded in putting a man on the inside, it'll take more time for him to establish himself in a position of trust. We need someone who can testify that Deboque himself gave an order."

Alexander rose, needing to pace off the excess energy that came from swallowing his thirst for action instead of talk. Intellectually he knew Reeve was right. To successfully destroy Deboque would take time and patience. But emotionally... He wanted revenge, the grimly sweet satisfaction of it. Now, as always, he had no choice but to put his wants second to necessity.

"You have someone in mind?"

Reeve tapped out his cigarette. "I will have within a week."

"In the meantime?"

"In the meantime I suggest we continue to upgrade our security, keep Deboque's people under surveillance and prepare for his next move. It will come." He spoke first to Alexander, then shifted his gaze, cool and calm, to Armand. "And it will come soon."

Armand nodded. "I will leave it to you to contact Jermaine at the Paris embassy. Perhaps tomorrow you will have a report on your conversation with Linnot on palace security."

"Tomorrow."

"Good. Now, I could be allowed a moment to ask about my grandchildren." Armand smiled, and there was warmth in his eyes. His shoulders never relaxed.

"They're hellions."

The laugh came as both appreciation and relief. "I thank God for it. Perhaps one day our biggest concern will be that Damien has dug up the kitchen garden."

The knock came fast and hard. Armand's brows rose only slightly at the interruption, but his body was braced. Because Alexander was already standing, Armand gestured for him to answer. The moment the door was opened, Eve stepped forward.

He saw it immediately, the ice pale skin, the too large eyes. He heard the breath come quickly through her lips as he stood, half blocking, half shielding her.

"Alexander." She reached for him because the need and the gesture were natural. He was safe. She thanked God for it even as the sickness rose in her stomach at the thought of what might be.

Gabriella put a hand on her arm. "We need to speak with Father. Where's Bennett?"

"In Le Havre until tomorrow." Alexander needed no explanation. The look in Eve's eyes, the tone of his sister's voice were enough. Without a word he stepped back to let them through.

Eve forgot protocol and formal greetings as she hurried forward. She went directly to Armand's desk. He'd risen, but even through her nerves she saw he stood as prince, not as friend.

"Your Highness, I received a phone call at the center only minutes ago. You must release Deboque from prison within forty-eight hours."

The veil fell over his eyes—Eve could have sworn she'd seen it fall. "Is this a demand or advice?"

Before Eve could speak, Gabriella again laid a hand on her arm. "A warning was issued through Eve. She was told that if Deboque wasn't released, a member of the royal family would die."

Where was the emotion? Eve wondered as she watched the prince. Where was the fear for his family, for himself? He watched her calmly, then gestured for her to sit. "Alexander, I think Eve could use a glass of brandy."

"Your Highness, please, I'm not the one you have to worry about. No one's threatening me."

"Please, sit down, Eve. You're very pale."

"I don't—" But the slight increase in the pressure of Gabriella's fingers on her arm stopped the protest. She cleared the frantic words away with a long breath and tried again. "Your Highness, I don't believe this was an empty threat. If Deboque is still in prison two days from now, there will be an assassination attempt on one of you."

Alexander placed a brandy snifter in her hands. She looked up and, for a moment, forgot everyone in the room but him. It could be you, she thought with a sudden wave of terror. If he was killed, her life would end.

As soon as the thought jelled, shock followed. Already pale cheeks blanched. She looked away quickly to stare into her brandy. But she saw the truth. She loved him, had always loved him, however impossibly. Before she'd been able to deny it, block it out. Now that he was in danger, her feelings rushed from her heart to her head.

"Eve?"

She pressed her fingers to her eyes and waited for her head to stop swimming. "I'm sorry, I didn't hear you."

Reeve's voice was patient. "It might help if we had the exact wording of the call, or as close as you can remember."

"All right." It helped, somehow it helped, to strain her mind and back away from the less tangible. She sipped brandy first, hoping it would settle her. "First he asked for me by name."

"You're sure it was a man?"

She started to answer quickly, then stopped. "No. No, I'm not. The voice disturbed me right away because it was so mechanical. Not like a machine, but as though it were being run through one."

"Very possibly was," Reeve murmured. "Go on."

"He said . . . something like I was close to the royal family and I should tell them to heed a warning. When I asked who it was he said . . . 'a seeker of justice.' I'm sure of that. Then he said there'd be only one warning. François Deboque was to be released from prison within forty-eight hours or a member of the royal house of Cordina would die." She compressed her lips a moment, then drank again. "I told him only a coward delivered a warning anonymously."

She didn't notice the glint of approval in Armand's eyes as he sat watching her, or the hand Alexander laid on the back of her chair. His fingers stroked her hair, and though she didn't feel it, she calmed.

"He only repeated that it was a warning and a promise."

"What was the accent?" Reeve asked her. "American, European?"

As if to force the memory out, she pressed two fingers to her temple. "There wasn't one, not a noticeable one. The voice was very flat and slow."

"Did the call come through the switchboard?"

Eve used the snifter to warm her hands as she looked back at Reeve. "I don't know."

"We should be able to check that. If Eve's been used once, she may be again. I'd like to tap that phone and put a guard on her."

"I don't need a guard." She set the brandy aside with a natural arrogance that had Armand measuring her again. "No one's threatened me. Your Highness, it's you I'm worried about. You and your family. I want to help."

Armand rose again, but this time came around the desk. With his hands light on Eve's shoulders, he kissed both of her cheeks. "Your concern comes from the heart. My dear, we are grateful for it. You must allow us to have the same for you."

"I'll have the guard if it eases your mind."

Her grudging acceptance made his lips twitch even now. She was not a coward or a fool, but as strong blooded—even headed—as his own children. "Thank you."

If she noticed the irony, she ignored it. "What will you do?"

"What needs to be done."

"You won't release Deboque."

"No, we will not."

She could accept that, had expected no less. Capitulation didn't stop threats. "But you will take precautions? All of you?" Her gaze slipped to Alexander and held. For an instant, perhaps only a fraction of an instant, her heart was in her eyes. He thought he saw more than concern, more than simple worry. More than he'd ever wanted anything, he wanted to step into what he believed was there and smother in the warmth. Instead he stood where he was, bound by breeding and necessity.

"It isn't the first time, nor will it be the last, that the House of Cordina has been threatened." The pride was there; she heard it. But below that, shimmering just beneath, she heard the hunger for violent and decisive action. She didn't retreat from it, but turned.

"Gabriella . . ."

"Eve, we can't allow threats to rule our lives. We have a responsibility to our people."

"We belong to the people, *petite*." Armand's voice softened as he took both her hands. "The walls of this palace are not for hiding behind, but for defending from."

"But you can't just go out, go on as if nothing has happened."

"All that can be done will be." Armand's tone was firmer now, a ruler's. "I would not risk my family indiscriminately. We will not risk ourselves."

She faced a solid wall. Armand, flanked by Alexander and Gabriella. Even Reeve ranged himself with them. She thought of Bennett, careless, carefree Ben, and knew he would have stood just as solidly with them. "I have to be satisfied with that."

"You are as one of my own." Armand kissed her hand. "I ask you as a father, as a friend, to trust me."

"As long as I'm still allowed to worry."

"You have my permission."

There was nothing more she could do, nothing more she could say. No matter how close she was, she remained an outsider. "I have to get back to the center." She picked up her bag, struggling against the knowledge that she could do no more than that. She cast a look at Reeve. "Take care of them." With a quick curtsy, she hurried from the room.

Eve was halfway down the stairs, when she remembered she had no car. The small inconvenience had her pressing her fingers against her eyes and fighting back an urge to sob hysterically. Three deep breaths brought her back to order. Swearing, she decided that with the energy she had boiling inside, she could walk it.

"Eve. You don't have a car."

She stopped at the foot of the stairs and looked up at Alexander. Did he realize how solid, how powerful, how completely confident he looked? He stood like a warrior, more ready to attack than to defend. He looked like a king, more ready to punish than forgive. Like a man more ready to take than to ask.

As he came down the steps, closer, still closer, she realized that was what she wanted. The strength, the control, even the arrogance.

"I don't want anything to happen to you." Eve said it quickly, before common sense smothered the words.

He stopped on the step above her, rocked more than she could imagine by the breathless sentence. Her concern was a warmth that reached inside his skin and arrowed its way toward his heart. But he was a warrior, and his first move was always defense.

"My father gave you permission to worry. I did not."

It was fascinating to watch her eyes, eyes so blue, go to ice in a matter of seconds. "Then I promise, I won't offer it again. If you choose to take a dive into hell, I won't even bother to watch."

"You change from honey to vinegar quickly. Part of your charm."

"I won't offer charm any more than I will concern."

"I don't want your worry," he murmured as he descended the final step. "But more. Much more."

"That was all I was willing to give." He had her boxed in neatly between himself and the banister. She wondered how he had managed it.

"I think not." He cupped her face in his hands. This was what he needed, if only for moments at a time. To touch her, to challenge her, to forget there was a world outside the walls. "What you say with your mouth and what you say with your eyes are not always the same."

She wouldn't be obvious. She refused to be easily read. What she had felt that moment upstairs would be hers alone until she fully understood it. Perhaps the fact that she had felt it, and he had not, pushed her. "Have you forgotten Bennett?"

She didn't wince, wouldn't permit herself to, when his fingers tightened on her flesh. "You didn't think of Bennett when you were in my arms. When you're in my bed, you'll think of no one but me."

Was it fear that roped into her stomach or anticipation? She knew already, somehow, that in his bed she would find everything she'd ever wanted and more than she might be able to bear. She wouldn't buckle to him. If she could promise herself nothing else, she could promise herself that.

"I won't be ordered into your bed, Alex." With her eyes cool, her hands steady, she pushed his fingers away. "I won't come to you as long as you think I will be. You want your brother's lover." It hurt her, almost more than she could stand, so her voice was as sharp as shattered glass and just as jagged. "That's an old story, and one that never ends satisfactorily for anyone involved."

The accusation cut into him until the temper he warred against daily threatened to pour out. He stepped closer and found her as strong and straight as any foe a man could face. Desire raced with rapier swiftness through his system.

"You want me. I've seen it. I've felt it."

"Yes." She wouldn't deny it. But her eyes were level and challenged the triumph in his. "But like you, I've learned to put my wants behind what's necessary. One day, Alex, one

day you might come to me as a man rather than a symbol
One day you might come to me with needs instead of demands.''

Whirling away, she started down the hall. ''I appreciate
the offer—of a ride, Your Highness—but I prefer to go
alone.''

Chapter Seven

Damn the woman! That was a thought that had leaped into Alexander's mind more than once in a two-day period. She made him feel like a fool. Worse, she made him act like one.

He had never had any respect for men who used physical force to intimidate. Such men had no character and very little intelligence. Now it seemed he had somehow become one of them. No, there was no somehow about it, Alexander corrected viciously. It was the woman who had driven him to it.

When had he started backing women into corners? With Eve. When had he started entertaining thoughts of taking a woman whether she was willing or not? With Eve. When had he wanted a woman so badly she clouded his judgment and dominated his thoughts? With Eve.

It had all begun with Eve; therefore it followed that Eve was to blame for his bouts of irrationality.

Because he was a logical man, Alexander recognized the flaw in that deduction. When a man lost control, publicly or privately, he had no one to blame but himself.

But damn the woman, anyway.

Seeing the quick, ironic smile, Gilchrist, Alexander's longtime valet, let out a small, silent breath of relief. Moodiness was something he expected and accepted from the prince. He could gauge within a heartbeat when to speak and when to remain silent. He'd never have lasted ten years otherwise. The smile meant more temperate weather was due, however briefly. Gilchrist knew enough to cash in on it.

"If I may say so, sir, you've not been eating well the past few weeks. If you don't pay more attention to your diet, we'll have to take your clothes in."

Alexander started to brush this off as fussing until he hooked a thumb experimentally in his waistband. There was a full inch of give.

Damn the woman for making a wreck of him.

No more, he promised himself. The insanity stopped here. "I'll see what I can do, Gilchrist, before you and my tailor lose face."

"I'm only worrying about Your Highness's health, not the fit of your clothes." But, of course, he was almost as concerned about one as the other.

"Then I'll have to promise not to give you cause to worry about either." Preoccupied, he nodded for Gilchrist to answer the knock at his door.

"Your Highness." Henri Blachamt had been Alexander's personal secretary for eight years. Before that time he had served in Armand's retinue. Even with twenty years total in service to the royal family, he remained elaborately formal.

"*Bonjour*, Henri. What impossible schedule have you lined up for me tomorrow?"

"I beg your pardon, Your Highness, your day tomorrow is rather full."

He wouldn't sit, Alexander knew, unless the prince seated himself first. Patient, Alexander settled himself on the arm of a chair. "Please sit, Henri, I'm sure that appointment book is quite heavy."

"Thank you, sir." After seating himself with a few of the fussy little gestures he was prone to, Henri reached in his vest pocket for small, rimless glasses. He settled them on his nose, straightened them, adjusted them, in a time-consuming ceremony Alexander would have tolerated from no one else.

His affection for the older man was very real and hadn't dimmed since that moment twenty years before when Henri had slipped the young prince a piece of hard candy after Alexander had received a particularly grim lecture on decorum from Armand.

"You remember, of course, the dinner party at Monsieur and Madame Cabot's this evening. There will be entertainment provided by Mademoiselle Cabot on the piano."

"It isn't possible to call that entertainment, Henri, but we'll let it pass."

"Just as you say, sir." There might have been a glint of amusement behind the lenses, but Henri's voice remained bland. "Council of the Crown member Trouchet will be attending, sir. I presume he will wish to discuss the matter of the proposed health-care bill."

"Your warning is appreciated," Alexander murmured, and wondered if he would survive the deadly boredom of the evening. Unless he missed his guess, the redoubtable Madame Cabot would have him seated between herself and her reedy-voiced, heavy-handed and unmarried daughter.

If only he could stay home, sit in his own garden at moonrise. With Eve beside him. She'd smell darker, more exotic than the gardens. He'd pick a spray of jasmine for her and her skin would be softer, smoother, than the petals. Her eyes would be the rich, dark blue that tempted a man and her voice would pour, warm and fluid over his skin until he was driven to taste her. She would smile at him, for him, as her arms reached out....

Damn the woman.

Both valet and secretary braced as the prince's brows drew together.

"What of tomorrow?" Alexander demanded, rising to face the window. He saw the gardens and deliberately looked beyond them to the sea.

Henri rose automatically and balanced the appointment book on his open hands. "Eight o'clock breakfast with the President of Dynab Shipping. Ten-fifteen, a personal appearance at the opening of the Le Havre Seaport Museum.

One-thirty, you speak at a luncheon for the benefit of St. Alban's Hospital. At three-forty-five..."

Alexander sighed and let the rest of his day pass by him. At least he was home, he reminded himself. Plans were already in the works for his European tour that winter.

One day he would visit the moors of Cornwall and the vineyards of France as he wished, rather than as Cordina's representative. One day he would see the people and places as they were, rather than as they looked for a prince. One day. But not today and not tomorrow.

"Thank you, Henri, that's certainly thorough." His hands linked behind his back, Alexander swore at himself. It was hardly Henri's fault. In fact, the only fault lay within himself and his sudden restless yearning to be free. He turned and smiled as the old man took off his glasses as elaborately as he had put them on. "How is your new granddaughter?"

A hint of color came into Henri's cheeks. All pleasure. "She is beautiful, Your Highness. Thank you for asking."

"Let's see, she must be... three months old now."

"Three months tomorrow," Henri agreed, his pleasure doubling that Alexander remembered.

Alexander recognized it, understood that small things were sometimes the most precious, and cursed himself for being so abrupt with his staff over the past few weeks. He would have liked to lay his mood at Eve's door, as well, but found it firmly lodged at his own.

"Certainly you have a picture of her. Annabella, isn't it?"

"Yes, Your Highness." Almost beet-red now, Henri reached for his billfold, carefully tucked into his breast pocket. Alexander took it and studied the nearly bald, chubby-faced infant. She was no beauty, but Alexander found himself grinning at the wide eyes and toothless smile.

"You're a fortunate man, Henri, to have such a legacy."

"Thank you, sir. She's very precious to all of us. The Princess Gabriella sent my daughter the lace dress, which had belonged to young Princess Louisa. My daughter cherishes it."

"So she should, if anything survives Louisa." He glanced at the white lace around the baby's wide face. How like Brie to have been so generous. "Give my best to your family, Henri."

"I will, sir. Thank you. We all look for the day when you give Cordina a son or daughter. That, Your Highness, will be a day of celebration."

"Yes." Alexander handed back the billfold. Give Cordina. His son would be heir even as he was now. The bond, both exquisite and heavy, would never be broken. And the mother of his children would have to accept the rules that had been carved out centuries before. What he would have to ask of her could be no less than what he asked of himself. If he made a mistake in his choice, he would live with it always. There could be no divorce for the ruler of Cordina.

At thirty, Alexander was the oldest unmarried heir in Cordinian history, a fact that the press reminded him and his country of at regular intervals. Yet marriage was something he still refused to contemplate.

Henri cleared his throat deliberately to bring back Alexander's attention. "Your fencing partner will be here by five-thirty, Your Highness. You must be at the Cabots' by eight-thirty."

"I won't forget."

Ten minutes later, dressed in white trousers and jacket, Alexander walked down the main staircase. The tension he'd carried with him for days hadn't eased. No amount of logical thinking helped. The war remained inside him, raging. Duty against need. Responsibility against desire.

The front door opened as he reached the bottom step. He stopped, muscles taut, thinking of Eve.

But it was Bennett who walked through, with a young, very shapely redhead on his arm.

"I can't believe I'm going to get a tour of the palace." Though her voice was breathy with excitement, the diction was perfect. After a moment's study, Alexander recognized her as one of Eve's troupe.

"Are you sure it's all right?"

"Darling, I live here." Alexander heard the amusement in his brother's voice as Bennett stroked a hand over the woman's shoulder.

"Of course." With a nervous laugh, she looked at Bennett. "It's so hard to think of you as a prince."

"That's fine. Why don't you think of me as— Hello, Alex." Bennett straightened away from the woman and his smile was crooked. "Have you met Doreen? She just joined Eve's troupe before they left the United States."

"Yes, we met at the dinner last week. A pleasure to see you again."

"Thank you, Your Highness." On cue, she curtsied. Bennett had a moment to think wryly that she had no trouble seeing Alexander as a prince. "Your brother, ah, Prince Bennett, offered me a tour of the palace." She sent Bennett a glowing look.

"How delightful." No one but Bennett would have recognized the sarcasm in the dry tone. "Perhaps you'd like to see the parlor first." While Bennett looked on in confusion, Alexander took Doreen's arm and led her a few steps down the hall. "It's quite comfortable and some of the furnishings are seventeenth century. You can amuse yourself, can't you, while I have a word with my brother?"

"Oh, yes, Your Highness. Thank you."

Alexander watched Doreen wander toward the mantel and the Wedgwood before he strode back to his brother.

"Very smooth," Bennett commented. "Now why don't you tell me why you wanted her out of the way?" At Alexander's look, Bennett's heart stopped. "Is something wrong? Father?"

"No." Normally Alexander would have hastened to re-assure him. At the moment he had only one focus and one purpose. "How could you bring that woman here?"

"What?" Relief became confusion and confusion amusement. Bennett's deep, infectious laugh rolled down the ancient hallway. "Doreen? Alexander, I promise you, I don't intend to seduce her in the portrait gallery."

"But somewhere else, and at the first opportunity."

Bennett stiffened. He tolerated his reputation in the press and, a fair man, was willing to accept the fact that he deserved the title Playboy Prince to a certain extent. Elder brother or not, he wouldn't tolerate it from Alexander.

"If, when and whom I seduce remains my business, Alex. Try to remember you'll rule Cordina, but not me. Never me."

The fury rippled just under the surface of cool, biting words. "I don't care if you take one of the kitchen maids in the pantry, as long as you're discreet."

Bennett's innate humor didn't surface. "Perhaps I should take that as a compliment, but I find it difficult."

"Don't you care anything for her feelings?" Alexander exploded. "That you'd flaunt one of your—distractions here, in her face? And that you should choose one of her own people. I've never known you to be cruel, Bennett. Careless, even selfish, but never cruel."

"Wait a minute." Bennett ran a hand over his face and through his thick mane of hair. "I feel as though I've walked in on Act Two. Are you talking about Eve? You think she'd be upset that I'm, well, let's say flirting with one of her actors?"

Alexander felt the rage spill over for a man who had the sun and only insisted on courting lesser stars. "If you must continually be unfaithful, can't you limit it while she's under our roof?"

"Unfaithful?" Bennett shook his head. "Now I'm afraid I've missed Act Two altogether. I don't have anyone to be unfaithful to..." The words trailed off as the full meaning struck. He stared at his brother, then collapsed in uproarious laughter. "Eve?" He choked on another fit of chuckles and leaned against the newel, carved three hundred and fifty years before into the head of a cat. "I can't believe that you—" Bennett struggled for breath, pressing a hand to his heart as Alexander's eyes grew darker and darker. "I can take that as a compliment, brother, and a truly inspired joke." He draped an arm around the newel, ankles crossed. There was nothing he liked so much as a good joke. "Alexander, you of all people should know better than to believe what you read in the paper."

Rigid with fury, Alexander remained where he was. "I have eyes of my own."

"But your vision's clouded. You can't seriously believe there's anything... God, how to put this delicately." He ran his hand over his face again, then dropped it. The smile was still in place. "Anything intimate between me and Eve?"

"You can stand there and tell me you're not lovers?"

"Lovers? Sweet Lord, I've never even touched her. How could I?" Though the amusement still colored his tone, sincerity balanced it. "She's part of the family. She's as much sister to me as Brie."

Something twisted open in Alexander's heart, but he remained a cautious man. "I've seen you together, walking in the garden, laughing in corners."

Bennett's smile faded slowly as Alexander spoke. Comprehension came just as slowly. His brother loved, and because their family bond was strong, Bennett understood the torment it would have caused him. "Because she's about the closest friend I have, and one I see so seldom. There's nothing between us, Alex." He stepped closer, wondering how long his proud, stubborn brother had been hurting. "If you'd asked me sooner, I'd have told you."

The weight began to lift from his shoulders, the back of his neck, his heart. And yet... "Perhaps there's no attachment on your side. Can you be so sure of Eve?"

The grin returned, quick, dashing, confident. "Alex, if there's one thing I know, it's what a woman feels about me. But if you don't want to go with that, why don't you just ask her?"

"I have. She didn't deny it."

"To spite you," Bennett said with instant comprehension. "It would be just like her—and I'd also guess it had something to do with the way you asked."

Alexander remembered the way he had approached her, with cutting accusations and anger. No, she hadn't denied it, but had let him dance on his own hot coals. He couldn't damn her for that.

Alexander studied his brother again and saw that his feelings were no longer his alone. In youth they had shared a great deal, secrets, complaints, jokes. Alexander could only thank God they wouldn't share the same woman.

"How could you not want her?"

Bennett leaned back again and looked at his brother. Someone had finally pierced the impenetrable, shaken the unshakable. "I did. The first time I saw her, I thought she was the most delectable creature I'd ever met." At Alexander's narrowed look, Bennett chuckled. "Don't challenge me to a duel yet. Besides, if you challenge, I pick the weapons. I'm a better shot than you are."

"Why is it you seem to find this so amusing?"

"Because I love you." It was said with the simplicity of truth. "It isn't often enough that those who love you see you act human, Alex. If I didn't enjoy seeing Prince Perfect falter a bit, I wouldn't be human. I'd say this round of jealousy's been good for you."

The childhood nickname didn't irk him so much as the reference to jealousy. "I haven't had a decent night's sleep in months."

"Enormously good for you." Bennett picked a rose from a vase at his elbow, thinking it would complement Doreen's skin. "But to get you off this pin you're stuck on, I was attracted to Eve, and I like to think it was mutual. Then before anything could be done about it, I was flat on my back in the hospital. She came in every day.''

"I remember."

"Fussing and nagging," Bennett added. "Standing over me until I ate that pap they forced on me, lecturing me. By the time I was on my feet again, we were friends. We've never been anything else." He passed the flower under his nose. "Now if you're satisfied, I have a lady with incredibly long legs waiting for me." He started down the hall, then stopped and turned. "You've never been one for advice, but I'll give it, anyway. If you want Eve, don't circle around it. She's a woman for the direct approach, no pretty lies, no staged seductions. She's gold, Alex, solid gold, with a mind as strong and sharp as a scalpel. A man would have to recognize that unless he wants small pieces sliced out of him."

If any man he knew understood women it was Bennett. Alexander felt the first smile form. "I'll keep that in mind." He watched his brother disappear into the parlor. Seconds later, there was a delighted feminine laugh.

Alexander stayed where he was a moment, trying to absorb what he knew, what he felt. Not his brother's woman. Never his brother's woman. But his. From this moment. Alexander strode toward the east wing quickly, needing to expend the energy racing through him.

She'd had a hell of a day. Tired and annoyed with the world at large, Eve let herself in the east entrance of the palace. Only friends and family used the small, secluded garden entrance. Normally she would have come straight in the front, but at the moment, she wanted to see and speak to no one.

Her director was edgy, and it showed. Her actors were picking up on it and had been sniping at one another as often as they blew their lines.

As producer, she could dump a lot of the heartache on her stage manager. But, damn it, it was her company. She'd conceived it, nurtured it, and she just wasn't ready to cut the apron strings.

As a result she'd spent the past two hours in a full meeting, cast and crew, letting the gripes and misconceptions be aired.

The members of her company were mollified. She was wired.

Face it, she told herself as she closed the pretty, carved door at her back. You've been wound tight for weeks and it hasn't a thing to do with the company.

He was making her crazy—mind, body, soul. How was it he could go through the motions, day after day, night after night, as though nothing had happened between them? How was it he followed routine, apparently without a ripple, when she spent sleepless nights worrying about an anonymous phone call?

The time was up, she thought, and rubbed at her aching temples. Deboque was still in prison, would remain in prison. How long would it take before the threat she'd received became action?

She remembered vividly the picture of Bennett lying on the stone floor of the terrace, the blood seeping out of him and onto the dark rock. It took little imagination to see Alexander there.

She could lose him. Though she knew he wasn't hers, had never been hers, the threat of losing him clenched the muscles of her stomach. Whether or not he loved her, whether or not he trusted or respected her, she wanted him alive and whole.

And the forty-eight hours were up.

Perhaps it had been only a threat. Giving in to fatigue and nerves, she leaned back against the cool wood of the door and shut her eyes. The Bissets weren't taking it seriously. If they were, wouldn't she have seen extra guards at the gate? Wouldn't security have been tightened around the palace? Because she had checked personally, she knew Armand was in Cordina, meeting with the Council of the Crown. The rest of the royal family were keeping both official and social engagements as usual.

And the forty-eight hours were up.

Nothing was going to happen. Anything could happen. Why did it seem that she was the only one wrapped up in nerves?

Royalty! she thought, and pushed herself away from the door. Did they think that because their blood was blue it couldn't be shed? Did they think that a title worked as an invisible shield against gunfire? Even Bennett refused to listen to her. In fact, he wouldn't even discuss it with her. Trust them to bind themselves together in this. But all she could see was the picture of wagons drawing into a circle as Indians attacked.

Enough, Eve warned herself. She was through losing sleep over them, *all* of them. She had a company to run and plays to produce. She'd leave the Bissets to run their own lives and their own country.

Then she heard footsteps, whispers. And froze.

Her first reaction was quick and primitive. Run. Almost as it formed came another. Protect.

Eve braced herself against the wall, breathing deeply. Her legs spread, knees bent, her body turned slightly, she lifted her arms to complete the fighting stance. Warriors had used it for centuries when facing an enemy with no more than body and wit.

As the footsteps came closer, she drew her right arm back, her shoulders set straight as a ruler. She took one step forward, leading with her stiffened open hand. Her breath came out in a whoosh. She stopped a scant half inch from Bennett's straight, aristocratic nose.

"Damn, Eve, I didn't think you'd be that upset about me dating one of your people."

"Ben!" With muscles gone limp, Eve collapsed against the wall. She'd gone white as a sheet and he could do nothing but grin. "I might have hurt you."

Healthy masculine pride came to the rescue. "I doubt it. But what are you doing lurking around the corridors?"

"I wasn't lurking. I've just come in." Her gaze shifted to the young redhead. She should have known Bennett would have ferreted this one out before long. "Hello, Doreen."

"Hello, Ms. Hamilton."

Eve straightened her shoulders, then worked away embarrassment by brushing a speck of lint from her jeans. "Ben, if I'd followed through, I'd have broken your jaw. Why are you sneaking around?"

"I wasn't—" He caught himself on the edge of justifying his presence in his own home. Bennett shook his head, amazed that Alexander would mistake his relationship with Eve for anything like sexual attraction. "It seems I have to keep explaining that I live here. In any case, my jaw is safe. I'm showing Doreen the palace before dinner."

"That's nice." It was only a murmur as nerves flooded back. The hands that had been stiffened and ready to attack twisted together. "Is everyone else home?"

"Yes." Recognizing her concern, Bennett tugged on her hair. "Everyone's fine. Oh, Alexander is a bit out of sorts, but—"

"What happened?" Instantly her hands were clamped to his shirt. "Was he hurt?"

"He's fine. For heaven's sake, mind the material." If he'd had any doubt about Eve's feelings toward his brother, he had none now. "I saw him an hour ago," he continued as he pried her fingers from the freshly laundered silk. "He was a bit annoyed at my, ah, flaunting one flower in front of the other. If you get my drift."

She did, and her eyes narrowed. "Idiot."

"Yes, well..." To keep himself from laughing at his brother in front of Doreen, Bennett coughed into his hand. "I straightened him out on all counts. So the problem's solved." He smiled charmingly, glad to do them both a favor.

"Straightened him out, did you?" Now her eyes were slits, dark, dangerous slits. "You feel you had the right to speak for me?"

"For myself." Bennett held up a soothing, or protecting, hand, palm out. "I simply explained that..." He shot a look at a quiet, but raptly attentive Doreen. "Ah, that nothing had ever been—well, been." Uncomfortable he shifted. "It seemed to satisfy him."

"Oh, did it? Isn't that lovely." Eve jammed restless hands into her pockets. "I'll do my own explaining in the future, thank you." Her voice was honey with a dash of bitters. "Where is he?"

Grateful that the temper in her eyes was about to be pointed in another direction, Bennett smiled. His only regret was that he wouldn't see the results. "Since he was dressed for fencing, I'd say he's in the gym with his partner."

"Thanks." She took three strides down the hall before calling over her shoulder, "Rehearsal's at nine sharp, Doreen. I want you rested."

Eve had always liked the area in the east wing the Bissets had converted to a gym. She was a physical woman, and one who could appreciate the beauty and contrast of a room with lofted, carved ceilings and steel machines and weights. There was no scent of the sea here, no pretty cut flowers in crystal vases, but the stained glass windows were rich and ancient.

She passed through the exercise room. Normally she would have admired the first-rate equipment and setup. Now she did no more than glance around to assure herself the room was empty.

The tang of chlorinated and heated water hit her as she entered the solarium, where a red fiberglass spa dominated. Steam rose up; the sun poured in. Through the clear glass you could see the sky and touches of the sea with its deeper blue. Another time she might have been tempted to relieve her tensed muscles in the soothing water. Again she passed through with only a glance. And when she opened the next door, she heard the clash and scrape of swords.

The tall, windowless room had a floor of dull hardwood, spread now with the *piste*, the fencing mat, of linoleum. Along one wall ran a mirror and dance *barre*. Two men in white were reflected in the glass as they moved together, knees slightly bent, backs straight, left arms curled up and behind.

Both men were tall, both slim and dark headed. The mesh masks hid and protected their faces through the thrusts and parries. Eve had no trouble recognizing Alexander.

It was the way he moved. Regally, she thought with a sniff, and crossed her arms over her chest while fighting to ignore the quick surge of need. It would always be there when she saw him. She had to acknowledge, even accept it, and go on.

The room rang, metal on metal. The men were silent but for their breathing. And well matched, Eve decided as she watched and analyzed styles and movement. Alexander would never have chosen an inferior fencer as his partner. He'd want the challenge. Little thrills ran up her arms. And the triumph.

In another century, another life, he would have defended his country with the sword, wielding it in battle to protect his people, his land, his birthright.

He could use it still, Eve realized as he moved steadily forward, offense rather than defense. More than once Eve saw him drop his guard to attack, parrying his opponent's thrust just before the safety tip made contact.

Would he fight so recklessly, she wondered, if the points were honed sharp. Another thrill passed through her, this time to twist in her stomach as she answered her own question.

In this one-on-one he would indeed be reckless in the way he never allowed himself in matters of state. His outlet would be the physical, which she understood, and the sense of danger, which she did not.

Again and again he challenged his opponent. Swords crossed; metal slid whistling down metal. Then with two subtle movements of his wrist, Alexander was past the guard, pressing the safety button lightly to his partner's heart.

"Well done, sir." The defeated drew off his face mask. Eve saw immediately that the man was older than she had thought and vaguely familiar. He had a rakish face and an interesting one, lined at the eyes, shadowed with dark hair over the lip. His eyes were a pale, pale gray and met Eve's over Alexander's shoulder. "We have an audience, Your Highness."

Alexander turned and through the wire mesh saw Eve standing rigidly inside the door. He saw the temper, glowing in her eyes, stiffening her shoulders. Curious, he lifted the mask. Now his eyes, dark, still lit with the excitement of victory, met hers without obstruction. He saw, mixed with the temper, heightened because of it, the passion. The need. The desire.

Slowly, his gaze still locked on hers, he tucked the mask under his arm. "Thank you for the match, Jermaine."

"My pleasure, Your Highness." Under the mustache, Jermaine's lips curved. He was French by blood and had no trouble recognizing passion when he saw it. He would forgo his usual after-the-match wine with his friend and pupil. "Until next week."

"Yes." It was only a murmur. Alexander's eyes had yet to leave Eve's face.

Smothering a grin, Jermaine replaced his *épée* and mask on the rack before moving to the door. *"Bon soir, mademoiselle."*

"Bon soir." Eve moistened her lips on the words and listened to the door click shut behind her. Folding her hands primly, she inclined her head. "You have excellent form, Your Highness."

The softly spoken words didn't fool him for a moment. She was mad as a hornet and already aroused despite herself. But the words snapped his own tension. With a cocky grin, he lifted his sword in salute. "I can return the compliment, *mademoiselle*."

She accepted this with another slow nod. "But compliments aren't the reason I'm here."

"I thought not."

"I ran into Bennett." She would hold her temper, Eve promised herself. She would strangle it down and defeat him with cool, carefully chosen words. "Apparently you and he had a discussion." She moved farther into the room, strolling to the rack of fencing gear. "A discussion concerning me."

"A discussion that wouldn't have been necessary if you had been honest with me."

"Honest?" The word nearly choked her. "I've never lied. I have no reason to lie."

"You allowed me to believe, and in believing suffer, that you and my brother were lovers."

"That belief was your own." Suffer? How had he suffered? But she wouldn't ask. Eve studied the slim shiny *épées* and promised herself she would never ask. "I didn't choose to deny it because I didn't and still don't consider it any of your business."

"Not my business, when I've felt you melt and burn in my arms?" He examined the length of his own sword. "Not my business, when I lay awake at night dreaming of filling myself with you and hating myself for coveting what I thought was Ben's?"

"*What* you thought." She rounded on him, the softening his first words had begun, vanishing. "What, not even who. You considered me Ben's property, and now that you don't, do you believe you can make me yours?"

"I will make you mine, Eve." Something in the soft, solid tone ran a quiver down her back.

"The hell you will. I belong to myself and only myself. Now that you perceive your way clear, you think I'll tumble at your feet? I tumble for no one, Alex." She drew an *épée* from the rack. "You consider yourself superior to a woman because you're a man, and one with royal blood."

She remembered the times he'd held her and let her go. Because he'd thought she was his brother's. Not once, she thought grimly, not once, had he asked for her feelings, her wishes.

"In America we've begun to think of people as people, and things like respect, admiration, affection have to be earned." She cut the air with the slender sword, testing its weight. Alexander's brow lifted at the easy way she handled it. "If I wanted to be in your bed I'd be there." She brought the sword down in an arch that whistled with restrained power. "And you wouldn't know what had hit you." Now she saluted him. "Your Highness."

The ripple of desire tightened his muscles. She stood, dressed in black, her hair drawn back to leave her face unframed, a gleaming sword in her right hand. Challenging him.

He'd wanted her before. Now with his mouth drying up, he thirsted for her. Pride stung the air, coming from both of them.

"I have yet to ask you to my bed."

Her eyes were as dark and dangerous as the sea. For the first time since she had come into the room, she smiled. The smile alone could have made a man beg. "I wouldn't need an invitation. If I chose, I could have you on your knees."

His head snapped up at that. Eyes narrowed. The truth was too close to the bone. "If I decided the time had come for you and me, I wouldn't be on my knees." He walked closer, a sword's length away. "And you would tremble."

His truth was as sharp as hers. "The trouble is you've dealt with too many subservient women." On impulse she took down a mask and a padded fencing vest. "And with too few who'd dare to meet you on equal ground." Her smile was cool and determined. "I may not beat you, Alexander, but I'll see that you sweat for any kind of victory." Making up her mind at once, she slipped on the mask and vest. She walked to the *piste*, taking her position behind the *en garde* line. "If you're not afraid you might lose to a woman?"

Fascinated, he joined her on the mat. "Eve, I've been fencing for years."

"And took a Silver in the last Olympic Games," she acknowledged while her adrenaline flowed steadily. "It should be an interesting match, then. *En garde!*"

He didn't smile. She wasn't making a joke or an idle boast. He replaced his own mask, so that faceless, they measured each other. His reach was nearly half again as long as hers. They both knew it.

"What do you hope to prove by this?"

Behind the mask her eyes flashed. "Equal ground, Alex. Here or anywhere."

Extending her arm, she met the tip of his sword with hers. Steel, cold and slender, glinted in the mirrors. They held for a heartbeat. And lunged.

It was a teasing, testing start, with power held back. Each gauged the other's style and strength, but here Eve had the advantage. She had seen him fence before—today and years ago. At the moment, she would have cut out her tongue before admitting that she had taken up the sport because she had never forgotten how he had looked with an *épée* in his hand. Through every lesson, every match, she'd wondered if she would ever cross swords with him. Now the moment was here and her heart beat hard in her chest.

But her mind was cool. He preferred the attack. She'd seen this and contented herself with defense.

She was good. Very good. Pride and pleasure welled up in him as she blocked and parried. Nature prevented him from using his full skill, but even as he held back, he realized she made both a formidable and an exciting partner.

The slim black jeans distracted him with images of what moved so supplely beneath. Her wrists were narrow, but strong and flexible enough to keep him at bay. He moved in, challenging. Swords crossed and clashed between them.

For a moment they held there, close enough to see each other's eyes through the mesh. He saw in hers the same heated passion that ran through his own.

Desire tangled with the taste of competition. Her scent was dark and richly feminine; the fist covered by the bowl of her sword was fragile and he could just make out the glint of gold and sapphire on her finger. He wanted her here and now. The desire ground through him.

She sensed it—the longing, the passion, the fantasy. It called to something deep inside her. She wanted to hurl the sword aside, drag off her mask and his and surrender to the needs whirling in both of them. Would that mean victory for him, surrender for her? She thought not, and yet the suspicion of it drove her on.

Abandoning her steady defensive tactics, she attacked full force. Caught off guard, Alexander took a step back and felt the soft tip push against his shoulder.

Alexander lowered his sword, acknowledging the hit. "You had a good teacher."

"I was a good pupil."

There was something free in the sound of his laughter. It caught at her, tugged a smile from her. Then she realized it was a sound she heard much too seldom. His lips were curved behind his mask as he lifted his *épée* again.

"En garde, chérie."

This time he gave her the compliment of his full skill. Eve felt the change and her own lips curved. She wanted no concessions.

The room echoed with the scrape and clatter of steel. The mirror reflected them, one in black, the other in white, as they met on equal ground.

Once he nearly disarmed her. Eve felt her heart pump in her throat, and set for the next move. Her advantage was in speed and she came close to slipping through his guard a second time. But he parried, riposted and sent her scrabbling for defense.

Their breathing came quick and heavy. The desire to win clouded over with desire of a more intimate kind. One man, one woman, dueling. With or without swords it was as old as time itself. The excitement of the thrust, the thrill of the parry, the grandeur of the challenge.

Their swords met with a clash near the grips and their faces met through the sharp-edged vee. Breathing fast, blades tensed, each held their ground.

Then, in a move that left her uncertain, Alexander reached up to pull off his mask. It clattered as it hit the floor. His face was sheened with sweat; dark hair curled damply around it. But it was his eyes that had her bracing. Again he lowered his sword, then with a hand on her wrist, pushed hers point down. He drew the mask from her face and let it bounce beside him.

When he snaked his arm around her waist, she stiffened, but didn't pull back. Without a word he tightened his grip. The challenge was still in his eyes. The dare was still in hers. Her body met his, and she tilted her face up as he lowered his mouth. As she had with a sword, Eve met him with equal force.

The excitement that had stirred during combat found its release. They poured it into each other. She moved her hand to his shoulder, skimmed it over the slope and rested it on his cheek. The gentle movement was accompanied by a quick, catlike nip at his lower lip. He responded by dragging her closer. A sound deep in his throat rolled out and teased her questing tongue.

The sword slipped out of her grip. Free, her hand reached for him, working its way under his jacket to get closer, just that much closer, to flesh. The heat from his body radiated through the shirt and onto her palm.

More. She wanted more. More of the taste of him, more of the feel of him. More, much more of the heart of him. And more was too much.

She dragged herself away from him, from her own impossible wishes.

"Eve—"

"No." She lifted a hand to run it over her face. "There can't be a winner here, Alex. And I can't afford to be a loser."

"I'm not asking you to lose, but to accept."

"Accept what?" Torn, she turned away. "That I want you, that I'm nearly willing to give in to that, knowing it begins and ends there?"

He felt the tug, the fear. "What is it you want from me?"

She shut her eyes a moment, then drew a deep breath. "If you were ready to give it, you wouldn't have to ask. Please don't," she said when he started to reach for her. "I need to be alone. I need to decide just how much I can take."

She left him quickly, before she surrendered everything.

Chapter Eight

It wasn't a night for sleeping. The big, round moon shot its reflection in Eve's windows, lending silvery edges to the blue-and-white curtains. She had drawn them back, far back, but still the breeze ruffled the hems and sent them dancing.

Work had already been tried and rejected. Papers and files brought from her office littered her sitting room. She could hardly concentrate on costumes or ticket sales or blown bulbs when Alexander was lodged so firmly in her mind.

He was exposed, vulnerable. With Deboque still in prison, Alexander was at a dinner party. The foolishness of it had her dragging a hand through her hair. Disheveled from an evening of pacing and worry, it tumbled onto the shoulders of her short blue robe.

He was exchanging small talk over coffee and brandy while she roamed her rooms after a futile attempt to eat at all.

He'd gone out, she thought, despite the consequences. Despite everything. Hadn't that wild, groping kiss they had shared sent his system churning as it had hers? Perhaps she had been wrong, deeply and completely wrong, when she had thought the need had run rampant in him. If it had, how was it possible, even with his control, to block it out while he sat through a seven-course meal?

What was wrong with her? Weary of herself, Eve rubbed her fingers over her eyes. She'd been angry when she'd thought he had wanted her only to compete with Bennett, furious that he had wanted but held himself back because he'd believed she had slept with his brother. Then she'd been enraged because he no longer believed it and still wanted her. Now she was miserable because he might not want her as much as she'd thought.

What did *she* want? Eve demanded of herself. One minute she admitted it was Alexander, and the next she was drawing back, knowing there could be nothing lasting, nothing real between them. A man like Alexander would have to marry, and marry properly. He had to produce heirs. Royal heirs. Even if he desired her, even if he cared for her at all, he would have to look to the European Aristocracy for a mate.

Amazed that her thoughts were drifting in that direction, she shook her head. When had she started thinking beyond the moment, an affair, and toward permanency?

She knew about men—when they were attracted, when they desired, when they wanted only a toy for an evening or two. And she knew how to deal with them. Why was it she knew so little of this man? All the evenings and hours she had spent trying to find the answers, some key to Alexander, had resulted only in finding a key to herself.

She was in love with him. Even the little jabs of fear and the constant twinges of doubt couldn't diminish the scope of the emotion.

And she did fear. She was a woman who had been sheltered most of her life by an indulgent father, a pampering sister. The choice she had made only a handful of years before to strike out on her own had been made as much by whim as curiosity. There had been no real danger in it. If she had failed, there had always been the net of family and family money beneath her.

Even if Eve had squandered her personal inheritance, she would hardly have been left alone to flounder.

True, once she'd begun she hadn't thought of using her family to soften whatever blows she'd encountered. Her troupe had become the focus of her life and the success or failure of it personal.

She had succeeded, made something of herself through her own skill and sweat. Even knowing that, being fully confident didn't erase the knowledge that the risk had been slight.

With Alexander there would be no net to soften a tumble, and a fall with him would mean a nosedive, no blindfold, from a dangerous height. The risk was there, every bit as frightening as the temptation to take it.

If she stepped off the edge and counted on survival, she was a fool. But something told her that if she played it safe and kept her feet firmly planted, she was an even bigger fool.

Caught between common sense and feelings, she dropped to the window seat and let the sea air cool her skin.

He wasn't sure he could survive another night. His rooms were quiet, in sound, in mood. They had been decorated in greens and ivories, cool against warmth, with paintings of the sea and shore dominating the walls. Calm seas in his bedroom where he came most often to be alone and think. The sitting room beyond had deeper colors, more vivid hues. It was there, rather than his office or the family rooms, that he most often entertained friends. It was large enough for an intimate dinner or a competitive game of cards.

Shirtless and shoeless, Alexander paced the bedroom now in an effort to reign in the emotions that had haunted him throughout the long, tedious dinner and entertainment. His fists strained against the soft linen of his trousers as he shoved them into his pockets.

No, he wasn't sure he could make it through another night.

She was only a matter of rooms away, a dozen walls he'd already passed through countless times in his imagination. Sleeping. He thought she would be sleeping now as the clocks in the palace readied to strike twelve.

Nearly midnight and she slept. She slept and he wanted. He ached. No amount of training, no sacrifices, no studying had ever prepared him for the dull, constant ache this woman could bring to him.

Could she feel it? He prayed that she could so he wouldn't suffer alone. He wanted her to feel the pain. He wanted to protect her from all hurts. But tonight, dear God, tonight he simply wanted.

It was a wanting that had grown with the years, heightened, turned edgy. There had been times when he'd told himself the need would dissipate. Times when he'd believed it. Months would pass when he wouldn't see her—though he would still wake in the early hours alone, her face just at the tip of his consciousness. He could fight that back, smother the longing that seemed so nebulous in the face of obligations, responsibilities and a backbreaking schedule.

But whenever she was here, close enough to touch, the longing was no longer vague and was impossible to fight.

Now that he had touched her, tasted her, teased himself with fractions of his own fantasies, was he supposed to deny himself the rest?

How could he go to her when what he offered would be a lifetime of subterfuge or a lifetime of sacrifice? As his mistress he would never be able to recognize her publicly as more than a family friend. As his wife...

Alexander pressed his thumb and forefinger to his closed eyes. How could he ask marriage of her? He would always be tied to his country, his duty. So would whatever wife he chose. How could Eve, with her independence and strength, ever accept the restrictions that went with his title? He would have to ask her to give up country, privacy, career. He would have to ask her to subject herself to the fishbowl, the sometimes dangerous fishbowl, in which he had been born. How could he expect her to have the same pride, the same love for Cordina as he? How could he ask her for a lifetime at all?

But he could ask her for a night. One night.

If she would give him that, perhaps it would be enough.

Alexander stared out the window, the one that faced the same garden, the same sea, the same sky as Eve's. He would have one night, and then, somehow, he would survive an eternity of others.

He didn't knock. Such was his arrogance. The door opened without sound, but she sensed him before it clicked shut behind him. Such was his presence.

She didn't jolt. Such was her pride. Eve remained on the window seat and turned her head slowly from the night to Alexander. She'd known sometime during her contemplation of the sky that he would come. What had been denied, struggled against, wished for, would be met tonight. Through her own vigil, she had made her peace with that. They stayed with the room between them, while the air hummed, then settled.

"I won't rise and curtsy," she said in a surprisingly strong voice.

His brow lifted, in amusement or surprise, she couldn't be sure. "I won't go to my knees."

She felt a tremor dance up her spine, but her hands were steady when she folded them in her lap. "Equal ground?"

His stomach was knotted with tension, desire, but a strange and novel euphoria swam into his head. "Equal ground."

She looked at her hands a moment, so calm and still in her lap, then lifted her gaze to his. His stance was straight, almost unbending, but his eyes were anything but distant. There was so much she knew, so much she'd yet to understand. "Once I believed you wanted me because you thought Bennett and I were lovers."

"Once I despised myself for wanting you because I thought you and Bennett were lovers."

The cool, matter-of-fact tone had her pressing her lips together. Yes, he would have hated himself. She'd been a fool not to understand that. He had suffered. She no longer had to ask how. "And now?"

"I could say I'm relieved to know it's not so, but it would make no difference. Even honor suffers."

Honor. With him it would be as vital as the blood in his veins. She had the power to make him compromise it. She had enough love to see that he didn't. She rose then, but even with her hands still folded, looked anything but meek. "I can't take that as flattery, Alexander."

"It wasn't meant to flatter. I could tell you that you're beautiful." His gaze roamed over her face. "More beautiful to me than any other woman. I could tell you that your face haunts my dreams and troubles my days, and that yearning for you empties me. None of it would be meant to flatter."

At each word her heartbeat accelerated, until now it echoed in her ears. With an effort she stayed where she was, when her heart urged her to open her arms and offer everything. Equal ground, she reminded herself. Honor for both. There was no talk of love.

"Maybe it's best if you said nothing." She managed to smile, and even tilted her head. "Except to tell me why you've come."

"I need you."

The words rocked her no less than they rocked him. There was silence while the air seemed to absorb them. He saw it in her eyes, the astonishment, the softening, the acceptance. Moonlight shot through the glass at her back, so that she looked as though she might be a part of it—and still out of reach.

Then she held out her hand.

Their fingers met, steadied, then curled into one another. Contact was made, and the time for words was over.

Her eyes on his, she lifted his hand and touched her lips where their fingers joined. Silence.

His gaze remained locked on hers as he turned their joined hands over and pressed his lips to her palm. Still no words.

With her fingertips she traced the line of his jaw, touching now what she'd never felt she'd had the right to touch.

His skin was warm, warmer than the breeze that stirred at the curtains. There was no need to speak.

He used his knuckles to trace the curve of her cheek to her temple, then his fingers spread to comb through her hair, lingering—lingering over it as he had once dreamed of doing. The clock struck the hour. It was midnight.

No words, but feelings nurtured in secret for so long bloomed at last in the first moments of the new day. Desires, refused, denied, were now accepted in the shadowed moonlight of a day just ended.

There were things he wouldn't ask, and more she couldn't admit. So they came together without questions, emotions only, as the bravest of lovers do.

Her arms opened. Her mouth lifted. His arms encircled. His mouth lowered. Body to body, they drew out and drew on the first kiss of the morning.

The tenderness remained somehow, though the excitement thrummed just beneath. There was more than just desire now—a breath of completion for something started long before. Tonight. At last.

The air sweetened with her sigh as she allowed herself the freedom of a wish. The kiss was deep, thorough, awash with the anticipation that poured from each. Then his lips brushed hers lightly, not teasing but promising of delights and demands yet to come. When she trembled as he'd once predicted she would, he felt not the thrill of victory but a gratitude that her need was as sharp as his own.

He ran his hands over the silk on her shoulders, her arms, her back, tormenting himself with visions of what was concealed beneath. So many times he had imagined her. When he drew the silk aside, letting it slither and whisper and pool at her feet, he discovered his imagination was no match for the reality of her, naked and close with moonlight cloaking her.

A poet would have had the words. A musician could have played the tune that streamed inside his head. But he was a prince who had never felt himself more of a mortal man than now, watching his woman shimmer in moonbeams before him.

She didn't need poems or a song. What she saw in his eyes told her she more than pleased him. He would never give her beautiful, melodious words, but a look from him said so much more. With a smile, she stepped into his arms again and pressed her lips to his heart.

It beat so fast, so strong. For a moment she closed her eyes tightly, as if to capture the feeling inside her. His skin was bronze against her ivory. Fascinated with the contrast, she stroked her fingers over him, then spread her palm wide on the plane of his chest. His fingers closed over her wrist as her touch sent arrows of need through him. He felt the trip-hammer of her pulse before she drew her arm away to lock both hands behind his head.

Flesh heated against flesh; mouth hungered against mouth. Her tongue skimmed over his lips, then dipped inside for the darker, richer tastes.

More. Again the craving for more tore at her. But this time she would have it. She found the clasp of his slacks, delighting in the quiver of his stomach as her fingers brushed his skin. The moment hung, then raced by. And he was naked with her.

She, too, had dreamed of this, and now discovered that dreams would never be enough.

He gathered her up and held her in his arms, just held her as she pressed her face to his throat, wound her arms around his neck. The wind shivered at the windows as they lowered themselves to the bed.

The mattress gave beneath them with only a whisper. The sheets rustled. He buried his face in her hair and let her scent slice holes in his control. She flowed against him, not just pliant but willing.

A touch and a tremor. A taste and a sigh. Slowly, savoring, shivering, they discovered each other. She was so soft here, so firm there. The strength in someone so small never failed to astonish him. Fragrant. Her skin was a garden of delight to all his senses. If he ran his tongue over it, he could taste both passion and delicacy.

How was it she had never understood the compassion, the gentleness, the goodness in him? Yet she'd loved him, anyway. Discovering it all now, she was swamped by feelings deeper than she had believed herself capable of. Here was a patience she'd never seen. A sweetness she had never dreamed of. He gave it all to her, without her ever having to ask. He gave her touches of romance she thought herself too wise to need.

It wouldn't always be like this. No, she knew that. There would be demands, greed, recklessness. That she could accept when the time came. But this time, this first time, he seemed to know she wanted gentleness. More, much more important, he seemed to want it, too.

So her hands caressed. Her lips lingered. She showed him she could cherish as well as be cherished. Even when their breath began to merge together in shudders, there was no rage to complete. Prolong. Only to prolong.

When he filled her, they moved together without the haste of first passions. This was a hunger that had waited seven years to be sated. Together they burrowed in a beauty that came as quietly and as inevitably as a sunrise.

The moonlight still glowed. The curtains still billowed. Apparently the world had decided to go on with routine though everything had changed. The sheets were rumpled at the base of the bed, untended and unneeded as the man and woman fed off each other's warmth.

Eve lay with her head on Alexander's shoulder, a place that seemed to have been reserved for her. A place she'd never thought she would claim. His heart beat, still far from steadily, under her hand. His arm was around her, holding her close, and though she knew he was as awake and aware as she, there was a peace between them that had never existed before.

Had love done it, or the act of love? She didn't know, and wondered if it should matter. They were together.

"Seven years." Her sigh was long and shimmered through the silence. "I've wanted this for seven years."

He lay still a moment while her words were slowly absorbed. His fingers trailed over her face, then under her chin so that he could lift her face to his. His eyes were so dark, and this time the caution in them made her smile. "All along? From the beginning?"

"You were dressed like a soldier, an officer, and the room was filled with beautiful women, dashing men, just like a dream. But I kept seeing you." She wasn't ashamed of it, nor did she regret not telling him before. They had needed the years between. "There were flowers. The room smelled like springtime. And there were those dazzling lights from the chandeliers. Silver platters, wine in crystal, violins. You had a sword at your side. I wanted so badly for you to ask me to dance. For you to notice me."

"I noticed you," he murmured, and pressed a kiss to her brow.

"You did scowl at me once, now that you mention it." She smiled and shifted so that she ranged just above him. "And you waltzed with that lovely blond woman with the English complexion. I've hated her ever since."

He grinned and traced Eve's smile with his fingertip. How incredible it was to be relaxed, to be alone, to be only a man. "I don't even remember who she was."

"I do. It was—"

"But I remember that you wore a red dress with the back draped low and your arms bare. You wore a bracelet here." He brought her wrist to his lips. "A thick gold band with a smattering of rubies. All I could think was that one of your lovers had given it to you."

"My father," she murmured, stunned to learn he had noticed, had felt something. "In gratitude and relief when I graduated. You do remember." Her breath came out on a laugh as she tossed her hair back. "You did notice."

He no longer felt the weight, the twist of guilt or the denial. There was only pleasure, with himself, with her. "And from the moment I did, you've never been out of my mind."

She hoped it was true. Reckless, she didn't care if it wasn't. "You never asked me to dance."

"No." He twined a lock of her hair around his finger. "I'd already decided that if I touched you it might be the end of my sanity. I saw you leave the ballroom with Bennett."

"Were you jealous?" She caught her bottom lip between her teeth to try to suppress the smile.

"Jealousy is a very low and common emotion." He slipped a hand down to the curve of her hip. "I was eaten with it."

Her laughter was rich and full. "Oh, Alex, I'm so glad. There was never any need, but I'm so glad."

"I nearly followed you." He said this quietly as his expression turned inward. "I told myself I'd be a fool, but if I had—"

"No." She laid her fingertips on his lips. "You couldn't know what would happen."

He brushed his lips over her fingers, then took them in his. "I saw you come back in, alone, pale. You were trembling. All I could think was that Bennett had upset you. I reached you just as you were telling Reeve and my father what was happening on the terrace upstairs. You were as white as a sheet and trembling, but you led us back to them."

"When we got there and I saw the blood and Ben lying on the ground... I thought he was dead." She closed her eyes a moment, then lowered herself to Alexander. "All I could think was that it wasn't right, wasn't fair. He'd been so much alive." Even with her eyes closed she could see, so she opened them and watched the moonlight. "So long ago, but I've never forgotten any of it. When Janet Smithers and Loubet were arrested, I thought it was over and everyone would be safe. And now—"

"Everyone is safe."

"No." She lifted her head again and shook it fiercely. "Alex, don't shut me out of this. The phone call came to me, and the warning. I was there seven years ago to see what Deboque can do from his prison cell. I'm here now."

"It's not for you to worry about Deboque."

"Now you're treating me like a child, the way you think a woman should be treated."

He couldn't prevent his lips from curving. "You can accuse me of that when I have such a sister as Gabriella? Eve, I learned as a child not to expect a woman to like to be coddled. I only mean that you can do nothing about Deboque and that worrying about him is useless." He ran a fingertip down the side of her face. "If it makes you easier, I can tell you that Reeve is working on a solution."

"It doesn't. Every time you leave the palace to perform some duty I'm afraid."

"*Ma belle*, I can hardly remain in the palace until Deboque is dead." Seeing the expression on her face, he kept his voice quiet. It was best she understood, and understood now before they took another step. "Do you think it will end before that? As long as he lives he'll seek his revenge. It is in Cordina he's imprisoned."

"Then have him transferred to another prison."

"It's not so simple as that. Deboque knows how long and hard my father worked to put him behind bars."

"But Reeve said it was Interpol."

"And it was, but without my father's cooperation, without the information gathered by our own security, Deboque might still be free. My life, my family's lives can't be run on the fear of what one might do."

But hers could. Eve gathered him close again. "I couldn't bear it if anything happened to you."

"Then you'll have to trust me to see that nothing does. *Chérie*, where did you learn to fence?"

He was trying to distract her. And he was right. The night was theirs. It would be wrong to let Deboque spoil even that. "In Houston."

"Fencing masters in Houston?"

She was amused, and looked it. "Even America has room for elegant sports. You don't have to be embarrassed that I beat you."

"You didn't beat me." He rolled her onto her back. "The match was never completed."

"I scored the only hit. But if it tramples on your ego, I won't tell anyone."

"I can see we have to finish what we started."

She smiled slowly. In the moonlight her eyes were dark and lustrous. "I'm counting on it."

The alarm clock shrilled. Groggy, Eve groped for the button, then shoved it in with enough force to make the clock shudder. She could be late, she decided sleepily. This one morning they could get started without her. She rolled over to cuddle in Alexander's arms.

He wasn't there.

Still groggy, she pushed the hair out of her eyes as she sat up. The top sheet was draped over her, but it was cool, just as the sheet beneath was cool. The breeze still tapped at the hem of the curtains, still smelled of the sea, but now sunlight poured through. And the room was empty.

He'd picked up her robe and had put it at the foot of the bed. The bed they had shared. All traces of him were gone. Just as he was gone.

Without a word, Eve thought as she sat alone. She didn't even know when he had gone. It hardly mattered when. She reached for her robe before she rose, then slipped it on, belting it as she walked to the window.

Boats were already on the water, casting out for the day's catch. The cool white yacht was still anchored, but she could see no one on deck. The beach was deserted but for gulls and the little sand crabs she was too far away to see. The gardener was below her window, watering. The sound of his tuneless whistle reached her and quieted the birds. A trio of pale yellow butterflies rose up, fluttering away from the spray of water, then settling on already dampened bushes. Wet leaves glimmered in the sunlight, while the mixed scent of flowers trailed its way up to her window.

The day was in full bloom. The night was over.

She couldn't be sorry. There was no room in her heart for regrets. What she had shared with Alexander had been magic, a wish come true. She had found him gentle, caring and sweet. The glory of that still remained with her. Briefly he had held her to him as though nothing and no one mattered as much as she. Now that the night was over, there were responsibilities neither of them could ignore.

He would never ignore them, not for her, not for Deboque, not for anyone. She could stand at the window, struggling against the fear of what might be, but he would do whatever his duty demanded. How could she fault him for being what he was, if she loved him?

But, oh, how she wished he could be there with her, watching the morning.

Turning away from the window, Eve prepared to face the day on her own.

Chapter Nine

From the fly gallery above the stage, Eve had a bird's-eye view of rehearsal. It was in its sixth hour, and there had only been two bouts of temper. Things had settled down since the meeting she had called the afternoon before, but she continued to make notes on the yellow pad secured to her clipboard.

She'd been right about the casting, she thought smugly as she watched Russ and Linda run through a scene as Brick and Maggie. The spark was there, and the sex. When they were onstage the temperature rose ten degrees. Linda played Maggie the Cat to the hilt, desperate, grasping and hungry. Russ's Brick was just aloof enough without being cold, his needs and turmoils raging under the surface.

They were a constant contrast to the second leads, with the nastiness and rivalry not so much obvious as natural. She couldn't help but be pleased with herself, especially since they were going to bring the production in underbudget.

The director took them back, and Linda repeated the same line for the fifth time that hour. Both she and Russ went through the same moves. The patience of actors, Eve mused, and wondered at herself for ever believing she could have thought to be one. She was much better here, supervising, organizing.

But the set . . . she tapped her pencil against her lips. The set wasn't quite right. Too shiny, she realized. Too new, too staged. She narrowed her eyes and tried to see it her way. It needed to be a bit more wilted, used, even decaying under a sheen of beeswax and lemon oil. With a focal point, she realized with growing excitement. Something big and brash and shiny that would show up the rest. A vase, she decided, oversize and ornate in some vivid color. They'd fill it with flowers that Big Momma could fuss with while she was trying to ignore the disintegration of her family.

She scribbled hurriedly as she heard the director call for a break.

Maneuvering over ropes, she started down the winding stairs that would take her to the stage. "Pete." She cornered the property master before he could light his cigarette. "I want a few changes."

"Aw, Ms. Hamilton."

"Nothing major," she assured him, putting a hand on his shoulder and walking out onto the set. "Pete, we need to age things a bit."

He was a small man, hardly taller than her, so that their eyes were level when he turned and began to scratch at his chin. "How old?"

"Ten years?" She smiled in lieu of an order. "Look, the family's lived here awhile, right? They didn't buy all this stuff yesterday. I think if the couch were faded—"

A long, suffering sigh. "You want me to fade the couch."

"Upholstery fades, Pete. It's one of those unavoidable facts of life. I think if you took off the cover and had wardrobe wash it a half-dozen times that would do it. And dull the gilt on a couple of the paintings. I don't want any scratches on the furniture, but... Doilies." Inspiration hit and she began to scribble again. "We need some doilies."

"And you want me to find them."

"Didn't you once mention that you were a scavenger when you were in the service?" She said it mildly as she moved to a different angle.

"You'd have made general," he muttered. "Okay, faded couch, dulled gilt and doilies. What else?"

"An urn." She narrowed her eyes as they swept the set. It had to be just the right place, not center stage, not too far downstage, but— "Right there," she decided, pointing to the table beside a wing chair. "A big one, Pete, with some carving or a pattern. And I don't want anything too tasteful. Red, really red, so it stands out like a beacon."

He scratched his chin again. "You're the boss."

"Trust me."

"Ms. Hamilton, none of us have a choice."

She accepted this without a blink. "Don't spend over thirty for the vase. We're not looking for an heirloom."

He'd been waiting for her to get to the bottom line. "You want cheap, you'll get cheap."

"I knew I could count on you. Now on the bedroom set, I think it would be effective if we had some jewelry, gold and a little tacky, left on Cat's vanity."

"Already got the bottles and that big box of dusting powder."

"Now we'll have the jewelry. If wardrobe doesn't have anything suitable, we can pick up something. Why don't you check with Ethel? I'll be in my office for the next twenty minutes or so."

"Ms. Hamilton."

Eve turned at the leg on stage right. "Yes?"

"I never did care much for extra work." He took out his cigarette again while she waited for him to go on. "Problem here is, I can see you've got a feel for it—the stage, I mean."

"I appreciate that, Pete."

"I'll get your doilies." He struck the match. "But I'm going to send one of the women out for 'em."

"I've always admired a man who can delegate authority." She suppressed the chuckle until she was out of earshot.

She never had been quite able to figure out what a man like Pete was doing in theater. It seemed to her that he'd be more at home roping cattle, but here he was. He guarded his props as though they were treasures, and knew the theater history of each one. There wasn't a doubt in her mind that within twenty-four hours she would have everything she'd asked for.

After pushing open the door of her office, she pulled the pins out of her hair. She'd worn it up for the sake of coolness and efficiency, but the weight of it had begun to pull. Letting it fall free, she stuck the pins in her pocket. Priorities being what they were, she went straight to the coffee maker and switched it on. Then, because she had a half a dozen calls to make, she drew off her left earring and dropped it in with the pins. Before she could sit and pick up the phone, it began to ring.

"Hello."

"The royal family has made a mistake."

She recognized the voice. The hand still in her pocket closed into a fist that snapped the back from the earring. "The royal family doesn't give in to threats."

The call was being tapped. She knew it and remembered through the first fear that her job was to keep the caller on the line.

"You'll have to tell your boss that he will serve out his term in prison."

"Justice must be served. The royal family and all those close to them will have to pay."

"I told you before, only a coward makes anonymous calls, and it's difficult to fear a coward." But she was afraid.

"You interfered once and your seven years of freedom may be at an end."

"I don't bend to threats, either." But her hands were damp.

"They won't find the bomb, *mademoiselle*. Perhaps they won't find you."

As the phone went dead, Eve stared at it. Bomb? There had been a bomb in Paris. Her hand shook lightly as she replaced the receiver. No, he'd meant another bomb, here, today. *Alexander.*

She had her hand on the doorknob when the full impact of the phone call hit her.

Your seven years of freedom may be at an end. Perhaps they won't find you, either.

The theater, she realized. The bomb was here, in the theater. Her heart in her throat, she pulled the door open and began to run. She saw Doreen first, showing off a bracelet to two other members of the troupe.

"I want you to get out of the theater, go back to the hotel, now, all of you."

"But the break's nearly over and—"

"Rehearsal's over. Get out of the theater and go back to the hotel. Now." Knowing that even a mention of a bomb would send them into panic, she left it at a clipped order. "Gary." She hung on to control as she flagged down her stage manager. "I want you to clear the theater, everyone, actors, stage crew, wardrobe, technicians. Everybody. Get everyone out and back to the hotel."

"But Eve—"

"Just move."

She shoved past him and onto the stage. "There's been an emergency." She lifted her voice so that it filled all corners. "Everyone is to leave the theater immediately. Go back to the hotel and wait there. If you're in costume, leave as you are and leave now." She glanced at her watch. When was it set? Would she hear the explosion? "I want this theater empty within two minutes."

She carried the authority. There might have been grumbles, there were certainly questions, but people began to file out. Eve left the stage to check the storerooms, the dressing rooms, anywhere someone might have gone before the announcement was made. She found Pete, locking up his precious props.

"I said out." Taking him by the shirt front, she dragged him to the door. "Leave everything."

"I'm responsible for all of this. I'm not having some light-fingered—"

"You're out in ten seconds or you're fired."

That snapped his mouth closed. Eve Hamilton never made a statement she didn't back up. His chin shot up and a dozen different rejoinders rushed through his mind. Wisely he left them there and started down the hall. "Anything's stolen, you'll have to make it good," he muttered.

"Let's just hope something's left," she said to herself, and dashed to the other doors. Each one she slammed behind her echoed more hollowly. She found one actor dozing in a dressing room and routed him in seconds. He was shoeless and groggy, but she shoved him out in the hall and in the direction of the stage door.

Everyone was out, she told herself. They had to be. She thought she could hear the ticking of her watch inside her head. How much more time? Time could already be up. But she had to be sure. She was about to dash up the steps to check the second level, when a hand fell on her shoulder.

Her breath came out in a squeak, and though her knees went weak, she whirled to defend.

"Hold it, hold it." Russ threw up both hands. "I'm just trying to find out what's going on."

"What are you doing here?" Furious, she lowered her hands, but they remained in fists. "I told everyone to get out."

"I know. I was coming back in from the break when everyone else came out. Nobody knew why. What's up, Eve? Is there a fire or something?"

"Just go back to the hotel and wait."

"Look, what gives? If this is your way of saying you didn't like this morning's rehearsal—"

"I'm not playing around here." Her voice rose as the last of her control snapped. There were beads of sweat on her temples and a stream of it down her back. Cold sweat. "I got a bomb threat. Do you understand? I think there's a bomb in the theater."

He stood where he was a moment as she started up the steps, then he was scrambling after her. "A bomb? A bomb in the theater? What in the hell are you doing? Let's get out."

"I have to make çertain everyone else did." She shook him off and sprinted up the rest of the stairs.

"Eve, for God's sake." His voice cracked as he raced after her. "There's no one left. Let's get out of here and call the police, the fire department. Whoever."

"We will—as soon as I make sure everyone got out." After she'd checked every room and shouted until she was hoarse, she was satisfied. Terror began to edge its way in. Her heart in her throat, she grabbed him by the arm and raced downstairs again. They were nearly to the stage door when the explosion hit.

"I'm pleased you could meet me here, Monsieur Trouchet."

"I'm always at your disposal, Your Highness." Trouchet took the seat Alexander offered, setting his briefcase neatly on his lap. "It was a pleasure to see you at the Cabots' last night, but as you said, such a gathering is not always appropriate for business discussions."

"And as the health-care bill is, shall we say, a pet project of mine, I prefer to give it the time and place it warrants."

Settled behind his desk, Alexander drew out a cigarette. He was well aware that Trouchet objected to the heart of the bill and that he was in a position to sway many members of the council. Alexander intended to see the bill put in force, with very few concessions.

"I know your time is valuable, *monsieur*, so we won't hedge. Cordina has only two modern hospitals. In the capital and in Le Havre. There are fishing villages and farms in outlying areas that rely solely on the clinics set up by medical personnel. These clinics, though never conceived as profitable businesses, have steadily been losing ground over the past five years."

"I am aware of that, sir, as are other members of the council. I've brought documentation with me."

"Of course." Alexander allowed him to pass neatly typed sheets, facts and figures, across the desk.

"Taking into account these documents plus the statements from several village doctors, it is my belief that the clinics will only remain in force if they are taken over and run by the state."

Though he knew what he would find, Alexander gave him the courtesy of looking over the papers. "When the state takes over, it also takes the pride and the independence of the individuals involved."

"And greatly increases the efficiency, Your Highness."

"People run the state, as well, *monsieur*," Alexander said mildly. "The state is not always efficient. But your point is well taken. Which is why I believe that with a subsidy, an allotment only, the clinics—medical personnel and patients—can retain both pride and efficiency."

Trouchet closed his case but didn't latch it. His capable hands folded on the lid. "Surely you can see that a compromise of this nature is fraught with pitfalls."

"Oh, indeed." Alexander smiled and blew out smoke. "Which is why I come to you, *monsieur*, to ask your help in filling those holes."

Trouchet sat back, knowing he was being offered a challenge, a position of importance and a request for surrender all at once. He ran a finger down his nose as he chuckled. "I have no doubt you could fill the holes yourself, Your Highness."

"But together, *monsieur*, we work for greater efficiency, and ultimately for the same end. *N'est ce pas?*" Alexander drew out a file of his own. "If we could go over these—"

He broke off, looking up in annoyance as Bennett burst in.

"Alex." He didn't so much as nod at Trouchet as the other man rose. "Reeve just phoned. There's been an explosion."

Alexander was up from his chair, his muscles rigid. "Father?"

Bennett shook his head. "Alex, it's the theater."

His face went white, so white that Bennett stepped forward, afraid he would crumple. But Alexander held up a hand. When he spoke it was only one word. At that moment his world was only one word. "Eve?"

"He didn't know." Bennett turned to Trouchet. "Please excuse us, *monsieur*, we must leave immediately." He went to his brother's side. "Together."

The council member gathered up his papers and case, but before he could shut the lid, he was alone in the room.

"How? How did it happen?" Alexander demanded as they rushed to the car. When Bennett claimed the driver's seat he started to object, then subsided. Bennett was right to do so. He would probably kill them both on the way to the theater.

"Reeve was only on the phone for a minute." Bennett peeled down the drive, with the royal guards close behind. "She got another call, something was said about a bomb— about them not finding a bomb, and..." But he couldn't say the rest, not when his brother was so white and stiff.

"And?"

"And they realized the caller meant a bomb in the theater. The police were there within minutes, five, ten at the most. They heard it go off."

Alexander pressed his lips together. "Where?"

"In her office. Alexander," he continued quickly, "she wouldn't have been in there. Eve's too smart for that."

"She worried for me, for all of us. But not for herself." He wouldn't let go, though there was a pain burning between his eyes and another eating slowly through his gut. "Why is it we never thought of her?"

"If you want to blame yourself, blame all of us," Bennett said grimly. "None of us ever realized Eve would be drawn into this. There's no purpose in it. Goddamn it, Alex, there's no purpose in it."

"You said yourself she's part of the family." He looked blindly out the window. They were a half block from the theater. His muscles began to tremble. It was fear, stark, raging fear. Before Bennett had fully stopped at the curb he was out.

By the stage door, Reeve stopped talking to two of his men and stepped forward to ward Alexander off. At his signal a handful of police shifted over as a shield. "She's not in there. Alex, she's in the grove around back. She's all right." When the grip of Alexander's fingers on his arms didn't lessen, Reeve repeated. "She's all right, Alex. She wasn't in the office. She was nearly out of the building altogether."

He didn't feel relief. Not until he had seen for himself would he feel relief. Pulling away from Reeve, Alexander rushed around the side of the building. His eyes were drawn to the blown-out window, the blackened bricks. Pieces of jagged glass littered the grass beyond. What might have been a lamp lay in a tangle of bent metal on the path to the grove. Inside was what remained of Eve's office.

If he had looked through the space in the wall where her window had been, he would have seen pieces of her desk. Some of the wood, torn into lethal spears, had arrowed into the walls. He would have seen the soaked ashes of what had been her files and papers, correspondence and notations. He would have seen the hole in the inside wall that was big enough for a man to walk through. But he didn't look.

Then he saw her, sitting at the verge of the grove, leaning forward on a bench with her head in her hands. Guards flanked her and the man who sat beside her, but Alexander saw only Eve. Whole. Safe. Alive.

She heard him, though he'd barely even whispered her name. A shudder of emotion passed over her face, then she was up and running for him.

"Oh, Alex, at first I thought he meant it for you, and then—"

"You're not hurt." He had her face in his hands, framing it, exploring it. "Anywhere, anywhere at all?"

"No. Unless you count knees that tend to buckle and a stomach that tends to turn to jelly."

"I thought you might..." But he couldn't finish the thought. Instead he pulled her close again and kissed her as if his life depended on it. The guards kept the reporters at a distance, but the picture would hit the Cordinian and international papers.

"I'm all right," she murmured over and over, because it was finally sinking in that it was true. "You're shaking as much as I am."

"They could only tell me that there had been an explosion at the theater—in your office."

"Oh, Alex." She held him close, knowing the hell she would have experienced not knowing. "I'm so sorry. We were going out the stage door when it exploded. As it turned out, the bomb squad was sending in men through the main entrance. When it hit we just kept going, and the police didn't find us until they started spreading out."

He held her hands so tightly they ached, but she said nothing. "And your troupe? Everyone is safe?"

"I got them out within minutes of the call. All but Russ, that is," she added, glancing behind her at a very pale and quiet actor. "I was going over the second floor to make certain I hadn't missed anyone, when he—"

"You? You were going over?" Now she did wince at the pressure of his hands.

"Alex, please." She flexed her fingers until his loosened.

"Are you mad? Don't you understand that bomb could have been planted anywhere? There could have been more than one. Searching the building is a job for the police."

"Alex, my people were in that building. I could hardly waltz out not knowing if they were all safe. As a matter of fact, I had to drag Pete by the shirt, and—"

"You could have been killed."

There was such bitterness, such fury in the tone, that her back straightened, though her knees had begun to weaken again. "I'm very much aware of that, Alex. So could any one of my people. Every one of them is my responsibility. You understand about responsibility, don't you?"

"It's entirely different."

"No, it's entirely the same. You ask me to understand, to trust. I'm only asking the same from you."

"Damn it, it's because of my family that—" But he broke off as he gripped her shoulders. "You're shaking again."

"Shock." Reeve's voice came from behind. He had his jacket off and was draping it over her. "Both Eve and Talbot should go to the hospital."

Alexander swore at himself for not taking proper care of her, but before he could agree Eve was backing off. "I don't need to go to the hospital. All I really need is to sit down for a few minutes." Her teeth began to chatter.

"In this you'll do as you're told." Alex motioned for one of the guards to assist Russ.

"Alexander, if I could have a brandy and a quiet room, I would—"

"You can have a quart of brandy and as many quiet rooms as you wish. After you've seen Dr. Franco." He scooped her up in his arms before she could protest.

"For heaven's sake, I'm strong as a horse." But her head found his shoulder and settled there.

"We'll have the doctor confirm that, and bring in a veterinarian if you like." He paused briefly to look at Reeve. "We'll talk later?"

"I'll be at the palace in an hour or two."

Eve lay on the pristine white examining table and frowned as Dr. Franco shone the pinpoint light in her left eye. "Too much fuss," she muttered.

"Doctors like nothing better than fussing," he told her, then shone the light in her right eye. Flicking the light off, he took her pulse again. His touch was gentle, his eyes kind. Eve had to smile at the smooth white dome of his head.

"Don't you consider it a waste of your time to examine a perfectly healthy patient?"

"I need the practice." His lips curved in the bed of his white beard. "Once I've satisfied myself, I can set the prince's mind at rest. I don't think you'd like to worry him."

"No." She sighed as he attached the blood pressure cuff. "I just don't care for hospitals." Meeting the irony in his eyes, she sighed again. "When I lost my mother, we spent hours in the waiting room. It was a slow, painful process for all of us."

"Death is hardest on those left behind—just as illness is often more difficult for the healthy." He understood her aversion to hospitals, but remembered that when Prince Bennett had been recovering from his wounds, she had come every day to sit with him. "You've had a shock, my dear, but you're strong and resilient. You'd be pleased if I assured the prince you didn't have to remain overnight."

She was already sitting up. "A great deal more than pleased."

"Then a bargain must be struck," he added, gently coaxing her back down.

"Ah, the kicker." She smiled again and tried to ignore the fact that she felt like a bowl of gelatin. "How about free orchestra seats to opening night of each play?"

"I wouldn't refuse." Her pulse was strong, her blood pressure well within the normal range, but there was still a lack of color in her cheeks and a hollow look around the eyes. "But to seal this bargain, I must have your word that you will rest for twenty-four hours."

"Twenty-four? But tomorrow I have to—"

"Twenty-four," he repeated in his mild, implacable tone. "Or I will tell the prince that you require a night of observation here at St. Alban's."

"If I have to stay in bed all day tomorrow, I'll need more than a hospital."

"We could perhaps compromise with a walk in the garden, a drive by the sea. But no work, my dear, and no stress."

She could make calls from her bedroom, she decided. Her office would probably take days to repair in any case. And if agreement got her out, she'd agree. "Twenty-four hours." She sat up again and offered her hand.

"Come, then. I'll take you out before there is a rut in the corridor from the pacing."

Alexander was indeed pacing when Dr. Franco brought her out of the examining room. Bennett was leaning against the wall, watching the door. As soon as they came through, both men started forward. Alexander took Eve's hand, but looked at Franco.

"Doctor?"

"Miss Hamilton is naturally a bit shaken, but has a strong constitution."

"I told you," she said smugly.

"However, I have recommended twenty-four hours of rest."

"Not bed rest," Eve put in.

"No," Franco agreed with a smile. "Not complete bed rest. Though all activity should be relaxing. What she needs now is some quiet and a good meal."

"Medication?" Alexander asked.

"I don't believe she requires anything, Your Highness, but a bit of pampering. Oh, and I would disconnect the phone in her room for the next twenty-four-hour period." When Eve's mouth fell open, he patted her hand. "We can't have you disturbed by phone calls, can we, my dear?" With a final pat he wandered away.

"Sharper than he looks," Eve said under her breath, but was weary enough to accept defeat. "Russ?"

"One of the guards took him back to the hotel." Bennett touched her shoulder. "His nerves are a bit shot, that's all. The doctor gave him some tranquilizers."

"Now we'll take you home." Alexander took her arm. Bennett flanked her other side. "My father and the rest of the family are anxious to see for themselves that you're all right."

* * *

She was fussed over, pampered, as per doctor's orders, and put to bed by the Bissets' old nanny. The woman who had cared for Alexander's mother, for him and his brother and sister, and now for the third generation, clucked and muttered and had hands as gentle as a baby's. They were curled with arthritis, yellowed and spotted with age, but she undressed Eve and slipped her into nightclothes effortlessly.

"When your dinner tray comes, you will eat."

"Yes, Nanny," Eve said meekly as her pillows were fluffed and piled behind her.

The old woman settled beside her and picked up a cup of tea. "And now you will drink this. All of this. It's my own mixture and will put the color back in your cheeks. All my children drink it when they are sick."

"Yes, Nanny." Even Prince Armand had never awed her as much as the silver-haired, black-clad old woman with the Slavic accent. Eve sipped at the mixture, expecting the worst, and was surprised by a nutty herbal taste.

"There." Pleased with herself, Nanny nodded. "Children always think medicine will taste nasty and find tricks to keep from taking it. I know tricks of my own." Her stiff skirts rustled as she shifted. "Even little Dorian asks for Nanny's drink when he's feeling poorly. When Alexander was ten, Franco took out his tonsils. He wanted my tea more than the ice cream."

She tried to picture Alexander as a child, and only saw the man, so tall and straight and proud. "What was he like, Nanny, when he was little?"

"Reckless. Thunderous." She smiled and the symphony of wrinkles on her face deepened. "Such a temper. But the responsibility was always there. He learned it in the cradle. He seemed to understand even as a baby that he would always have more than other men. And less." As she spoke, she rose to tidy Eve's clothes. "He was obedient. Though you could see the defiance in his eyes, he was obedient. He studied hard. He learned well. Both he and Bennett were fortunate that their personalities were so markedly different. They fought, of course. Brothers must, after all. But they became fond of each other early as people.''

She kept a sharp eye on her patient, and noted the tea was nearly finished. ''He has the intensity of his father, sometimes more. But, then, the Prince had my Elizabeth to share with him, to soothe him, to make him laugh at himself. My Alexander needs a wife.''

Eve's gaze rose slowly over the rim of her cup. She was warm and growing drowsy, but she recognized the look in Nanny's eyes. ''He'll have to decide that for himself.''

''For himself. And for Cordina. The woman he chooses will have to be strong, and willing to share the burdens.'' Nanny took the empty cup. ''Most of all, I hope she is capable of making him laugh.''

''I love to hear him laugh,'' Eve murmured as her eyes fluttered closed. ''Does it show, Nanny? Does it show that I love him so much?''

''I have such old eyes.'' Nanny smoothed the sheets before she dimmed the light. ''And old eyes see more than young ones. Rest now and dream. He'll come to you before this night is over, or I don't know my children.''

She knew them well. Eve stirred and sighed and saw Alexander the moment she opened her eyes. He was sitting on the edge of the bed, her hand in his, watching.

''Nanny gave me a magic potion.''

He kissed her knuckles. He wanted to go on kissing her, holding her close and tight against him until the nightmare had faded completely. With an effort he kept his fingers light, as well as his voice.

''It brought the color back to your cheeks. She said you'd be waking soon and would be hungry.''

Eve pushed herself up. ''She's right. I'm starved.''

He rose and walked to a tray at the foot of the bed. ''She ordered your menu herself.'' He began to remove covers.

"Chicken broth, a small lean steak, fresh greens, potatoes mixed with grated cheese."

"Enough torture." Eve laid a hand on her stomach. "I haven't eaten since breakfast. I'll start anywhere."

"The broth, I think." He placed it on a tray.

"Oh, it smells wonderful." Eve picked up the spoon and began to recharge her system. He sat in silence while she worked her way through the soup. He could remember every word of Reeve's report.

Though tests had still to be run, it was almost certain that the bomb had been the same type as the one planted in the Paris embassy. If anyone had been in the office, or even within twenty feet of the door, it would have been fatal.

Eve's office—where he had once seen her sitting so competently behind her desk.

Security believed that Eve had not meant to be harmed. Hence the warning. The bomb had been used to terrorize, to confuse, to undermine. But if she hadn't been quick enough...

He wouldn't think beyond that. She was here now, unharmed. Whatever he had to do, she would remain that way. When she'd finished the broth, he removed the bowl and replaced it with the main course.

"I suppose I could get used to the pampering." The meat was pink and tender inside. "It was so sweet of everyone, even your father, to come in and see me, to make sure I was all right."

"My father cares for you. All of us do."

She tried not to make it mean more than it did. He did care. She'd felt it in the way he'd held her when he'd reached the grove. Maybe, just maybe, he even loved her a little. But she couldn't push him, or herself. It was best to deal with other things.

She toyed with her potatoes. "But I really do feel fine now, Alex. There's no need for you to go to the trouble of disconnecting the phones."

"It's already done." He took a bottle of wine from a bucket and poured two glasses. "There won't be any need for you to speak with anyone outside the palace tomorrow. Brie and her family are moving in temporarily. I'm sure the children can entertain you."

"Alex, be reasonable. I have to talk to my people. They must be frantic. You have no idea how overblown theater people can make things. And getting my office back into shape is going to take days."

"I want you to go back to Houston."

Slowly she set her knife and fork on the tray. "What?"

"I want you to take your troupe back to America. I'm canceling the performances."

She hadn't realized she had the energy for anger. "You try that and I'll sue your royal tail off."

"Eve, this is no time for ego. What happened today—"

"Had nothing to do with the theater and little to do with me. We both know that. If it did, I'd be no safer in Houston than here."

He was through with logic. In this, with her, there were only feelings. "I don't want you here."

The quick slice of pain hit its mark. She let it pass, then picked up her knife and fork again. "It won't do any good to try to hurt me, Alexander. I won't go, and neither will the troupe, not until all four performances are finished. We have a contract."

His French was harsher and a great deal more explicit than his English. He rolled into it as he rose to pace the room. She'd learned enough in her Swiss boarding school, particularly in the dorms, to understand him perfectly.

"Nanny mentioned that you had a filthy temper," she said, and continued to eat. The fact that she'd finally seen it loose pleased her. He wasn't so controlled now, she thought. So she would be. "The wine is excellent, Alexander. Why don't you sit down and enjoy it?"

"Merde!" He swung back to her, resisting the urge to fling her tray and its contents on the floor. "This is not a

game. Do you know what I went through when I thought you might be dead? That you might have been in that room when the bomb went off?"

She set her utensils down again and lifted her gaze to his. "I think I do. I go through much of the same every time you go out in public. This morning I stood at that window and thought of you. I didn't even know how long you'd been gone."

"I didn't want to wake you."

"I'm not asking for explanations, Alex." Her appetite gone, she pushed the tray away. "I'm trying to make you see what I was feeling. I looked out at the sea, and I knew you were somewhere, tending to Cordina. Somewhere I couldn't be, somewhere I couldn't help you. And I had to get dressed and go out and go on, when in the back of my mind was the fear that today would be the day I'd lose you."

"Eve, I'm so surrounded by guards that sometimes I think they'll smother me. The security on all of us has been doubled since the bomb in Paris."

"Is that supposed to comfort me? Would it comfort you?" He said nothing, but came and removed the tray from her lap. "You want me to run away, Alex. Will you run away with me?"

"You know I can't. This is my country."

"And this is my job. Please don't ask me to go." She held out a hand, watched him hesitate, then come back to take it. "If you want to be angry with me, wait until tomorrow. All through this hideous day I've wanted you to hold me. Please stay with me tonight, Alex."

"You need rest." But he gathered her close.

"I'll rest after," she murmured, and drew him down with her.

Chapter Ten

Her office looked as though it had been bombed. Somehow, even living through it, being told about it, reading the story in the paper, Eve hadn't been prepared for the stark reality of it.

She'd kept her word and had stayed away for twenty-four hours—mainly because she'd been given no choice. Now she stood at the doorway, or what was left of the doorway, and looked at what had been her office.

The debris hadn't been hauled away, by order of the police. They had sifted and searched through the ashes and rubble throughout the night of the bombing, the day she'd been kept away and the night she'd lain restless and anxious to get back to work. If there had been a sense of order to their investigation, Eve couldn't see it.

There was a hole in one wall, taller and wider than she, so that Eve could see that the small, unoccupied room beyond had problems of its own. Shafts of wood were burrowed into the plaster or lay heaped on the floor. Her file cabinet was a mass of twisted metal, the contents ashes. The carpet was gone, simply gone, with the floor beneath scarred and scored. The window had been boarded up so that no light seeped through. The repair crew was coming that morning, but she had wanted to see it for herself, before it was swept clean.

She didn't shudder. She had thought she would when she had been walking down the hall. The fear she had expected, had been willing to accept, didn't come. In the hole left by fear, anger came, ripe and deep and cleansing.

All her files, her notes, her records—destroyed. She stepped in and kicked aside a lump of ceiling. Weeks, months, even years of work reduced to rubble in a matter of seconds. Some things could be replaced; other things were simply irreplaceable.

The picture she had had on her desk, her favorite one of her and Chris; it was part of the ashes. Gone, too, was the play she had written and the one she'd been working on. The tears that sprang to her eyes weren't of sorrow, but of fury. Her work might have been rough, maybe it had even been foolish, but it had been her work. Lack of confidence and her own self-deprecating humor had caused her to file it away under *F* for Fantasies.

Now that dream was gone, blown apart by someone who didn't even know her. They had taken away pieces of her life, and would have taken her life, as well, without a second thought.

They would pay, she promised herself as she stood among the wreckage. Somehow, someway, she would see to it personally.

"Eve."

With the back of her wrist she swiped at her eyes before turning. "Chris!"

In that instant she was only a younger sister. The emotion and need swamped her as she scrambled over the wreckage and into her sister's arms. "I'm so glad you're here. I'm so glad."

"Of course I'm here. I came the moment I heard." Chris squeezed tightly as relief came and the hours of dread through her traveling eased. "I went to the palace first. I've never seen so much security there before. If it hadn't been for Bennett I might still be arguing with the guards at the gates. Eve, for God's sake, what's going on?"

"It's gone. Everything. The picture of us at the opening of my first play. It was on the desk. The little china cat Mom gave me when I was ten. I always took it with me. There's nothing left of it, nothing at all."

"Oh, baby." Holding tight, Chris surveyed the room over Eve's shoulder. Unlike her sister, she did shudder, for what might have been. "I'm so sorry. But you're safe." Anxiously, she held her at arms length to study carefully. "You weren't hurt?"

"No, no, I was nearly out of the building. Reeve said it was just a small plastic bomb. Not much range."

"A small bomb," Chris repeated in a whisper, and pulled Eve against her again. "Just a small one." Her own anger surfaced as she gave her sister a quick shake. "Eve, do you know how it felt to hear about it on the news?"

"I'm sorry, Chris. Everything happened so fast, and I guess I wasn't thinking straight. I should have called you."

"Damn right you should have." Then she let it pass, knowing what Eve's state of mind must have been. "Brie did. Prince Armand called Dad personally. He was all for hopping on the first plane and dragging you back to Houston."

"Oh, Chris."

"You're safe—only because I convinced him we'd have better luck getting you to listen to me."

"I'll call him. Honestly, I never thought the news would get to the States so quickly."

"I want the whole story, Eve, not the watered-down, public relations version I got on the six o'clock news." Chris's voice took on the firm maternal tone she had developed when Eve turned fifteen. "You can give it to me while I drive you back to the palace to pack."

"I'm not going back, Chris."

Chris stepped back and pushed her short, thick hair away from her forehead. "Now listen—"

"I love you," Eve interrupted. "And I understand how you must be feeling right now, looking at all this." She paused to take another scan of the room herself. The fury came back full force. "But I'm not running away. I came here to produce four plays, and by God, I'm going to produce four plays."

Chris started to shout, then checked herself. The one way you never got through to Eve was with orders. "Eve, you know how much I respect what you do, what you can do, but it's painfully obvious that Cordina isn't safe right now. This isn't worth risking your life over."

"The bomb wasn't planted for me. They only used me to get to the Bissets." She laid a hand on her sister's arm. "I can't go, Chris. I think once I explain everything, you'll understand."

"Then you'd better explain real good."

"I will." With a smile Eve kissed her cheek. "But not here. We'll use the theater manager's office." Eve urged Chris out into the hall, taking a quick look at her watch as they went. She intended to be back to work within the hour.

Twenty minutes later they were seated on a neat gray-and-rose sofa, working on their second cup of coffee. Chris drank hers black, using the strong, slightly bitter taste to soothe her nerves.

"Deboque." Her cup clattered in the saucer before she set it down. "All these years later and he's still causing such pain."

"From what Alex said he'll never stop." As long as he lived. Eve pushed the thought away. She had never thought she could ever wish anyone dead. "I don't even know what kind of man he is. Evil, certainly, and I'd guess obsessed. The person who called spoke of justice—he spoke of it both times. Deboque's kind of justice won't be met until Prince Armand is destroyed. Reeve thinks the bomb in the theater was a show of strength. Chris, what's really frightening is that I know—somehow I'm sure—that the next target is going to be one of the Bissets." She thought of Alexander and pressed her lips together. "It could be any one of them, even one of the children. That's why Reeve and Brie have moved back into the palace for now."

Chris was silent while her loyalties warred inside her. "Eve, you know how I feel about the Bissets. They're a second family to me. But no matter how much I care for them, you come first. I want you home, away from this."

"I can't leave. One of the reasons is the troupe and what we're trying to do here. Please hear me out," she continued as Chris started to speak. When she subsided, Eve rose. She had to move. Time seemed to be pressing in on her from all directions. "I have a chance to prove something here, to myself, to you and Dad, to my industry."

"There's nothing you have to prove to me, Eve."

"I do. You took care of me." She turned back, her emotions a little shaky. "You were only five years older, but when Mom died, you did everything you could to fill the void. Maybe I wasn't always aware of what you were doing or what you gave up to do it, but I am now. I guess I need to show you it was worth it."

Chris felt her eyes fill and quickly shook her head. "Do you think I've ever doubted it? Eve, I did nothing more than be your sister."

"Yes, you did. You were my friend." She came back to take both of Chris's hands. "Even when you didn't believe, didn't approve, you stood by me. What I'm doing here is as much for you as it is for me. I've never been able to explain that to you before."

"Oh, sweetheart." Chris's fingers tightened on hers. "I don't know what to say."

"Don't say anything for a minute. Just listen. A lot of people in the business chuckled behind my back when I first got started. Spoiled heiress out for a fling, that sort of thing. And maybe it was close to the truth at first. I never did anything worthwhile in my life before the troupe."

"That's not true."

"That's absolutely true." She had no problem accepting the truth, or using it to push herself further. "I skimmed my way through school doing the least amount of work possible. I lounged around during the summer doing nothing at all. I watched Dad wheel and deal, I watched you take your education and turn it into success with your gallery, and I picked up another magazine. With the theater I started to find a goal, without realizing I'd needed one. Chris, when I stood on the stage for the first time, it was like a light going on in my head. Maybe my place was behind it, not on it, but I found the goal. It took a couple years after the troupe was formed for people to stop laughing. Now I have a chance to do something extraordinary. I can't give it up.''

"I never knew you felt this way." Chris ran her hand over the back of Eve's. "I do understand, and I'm proud of you. I always have been, but I'm prouder than ever. I believe you can do something extraordinary, but the timing's off. Six months from now, a year from now, when things have settled down—''

"I can't leave, Chris. Even if they tore the theater down, if everyone of my troupe went back, I couldn't leave.'' She had to draw a breath to say it, to say it out loud and calmly. "I'm in love with Alexander.''

"Oh.'' Because the wind had just been knocked out of her, Chris said nothing else.

"I have to be with him now, especially now. Once I thought the troupe was everything, but as important as it is, it doesn't come close to how I feel about him.'' She paused a moment, realizing what she was saying had been there all along—she just hadn't known it. "You don't have to tell me that nothing can come of it—I've already figured that out for myself. But I have to be with him as long as I can.''

"Once I'd thought that maybe you and Bennett . . . I'd even gotten a kick out of imagining the two of you. But Alexander.''

"I know.'' Eve rose again. "The heir. I've loved him for years. I managed to do a pretty good job of muddling that fact, even to myself, but there it is.''

"I'd wondered a couple of times if you might have been a bit infatuated.''

"I'm old enough to know the difference,'' Eve said with a smile.

"Yes." Sighing, Chris sat back. "Does he know how you feel?"

"I haven't told him, but he's a very astute man. We've both been very careful not to mention any four-letter word beginning with *l*. Yes, I think he knows."

"How does he feel, Eve, about you?"

"He cares, perhaps more than he intended, less than I'd like. It's difficult to read Alex. He's had so much practice harnessing his emotions." She took a deep breath. "Besides, it doesn't matter."

"How can you say that?"

"Because it can't matter." She was a practical woman, or so she told herself. A realist. "I said I knew nothing could come of it, and I can deal with that. I'm a professional. My career takes a great deal of my time and energy. Even if Alex weren't who he is, I doubt if we could come to terms. I don't have time for marriage and a family. I don't need them."

"I'm going to take more convincing than that—and so are you."

"I really don't." How many times had she given herself this lecture over the past week? "A great many women don't want marriage. Look at you."

"Yeah." With a low laugh Chris sat up again. "Eve, the only reason I'm not married and the mother of six is that I never met a man who was more important to me than my work. You've already told me you have."

"It doesn't matter. It can't matter." There was a thread of panic in her voice. "Chris, don't you see that whatever I want, whatever I'd like, I have to deal with the reality. If I don't accept the way things are, I'll lose. More than anything else, I don't want to lose him. I will one day." Restless, she ran her hands through her hair. "He'll have to marry, start a family. It's a duty he'd never shirk. But until then I can share some part of him."

"You love him so much," Chris murmured. "I don't know whether to cry for you or be happy."

"Be happy. There are enough reasons for tears in the world."

"All right, then." She stood and wrapped her arms around her sister. "I am happy for you." And she reserved the right to believe dreams could come true. "I don't suppose you'd take the afternoon off and go shopping with me?"

"Oh, I can't. I have to get on the phone to Houston and have copies of my records shipped over. I should already be at rehearsal making sure everyone's calm. I have to find some office space around here." She paused, though her mind was clicking off the next steps. "Shopping for what?"

"I only brought an overnight bag. Arrogance," she said as she picked up the leather tote. "I was sure we'd be on a plane by dinner. Now, it seems, I have to see if Cordina has something sensational for me to wear to opening night."

"You're staying."

"Of course. Think I can wheedle a room at the palace?"

Eve gave her a bone-crushing squeeze. "I'll put in a good word for you."

Hours later, Eve sat at the portable typewriter in her sitting room. The day had gone quickly, filled with problems to be solved, but the evening had dragged. Alexander hadn't come back for dinner.

Bennett had been there, but even with his jokes and easy manner he had obviously been preoccupied. Reeve and Armand had also been absent. It was a family meal, with Gabriella and her children, Bennett, Eve and Chris—and the empty chairs where the rest of the family should have been. The moment the meal had been over Bennett had excused himself. The tension even his casualness hadn't disguised remained in full force.

When Eve mentioned the work she still had to catch up on, Chris accompanied Gabriella upstairs to tend to the children. Back in her rooms, alone, Eve tried to fill the rest of her evening with work.

Her four scripts for the upcoming productions had been destroyed, but new copies had been secured before noon. There was no reason to look over them. She knew every word, every bit of staging. If it had been necessary, she could have filled in for any of her actors on opening night.

The opening was only days away, and though the cast had been understandably edgy that afternoon, rehearsals had gone well enough. The second production was almost as polished as the first, and rehearsals on the third play would begin the following week. If there were no more incidents.

The house was sold-out for the first three performances, and ticket sales were mounting steadily. Pete had even managed to come up with the props she had asked for.

She'd thought about reviewing her budget, but the idea of tallying figures had been anything but appealing. She had looked at her watch, soaked in the tub and checked the time again. It had been nearly ten when she'd sat down at the typewriter, telling herself that Alexander was safe and well, probably asleep in his own bed after a difficult day.

She would work. Her own plays had been destroyed. She could only blame herself for not making extra copies. Maybe it was just as well. That's what she told herself. The first one had been too emotional and flowery in any case. The second—well, that had taken her six months and she'd barely gotten out of Act One.

So she'd start fresh. A new idea, a new mood, and in some ways, a new woman. Act One, Scene One, Eve told herself as she rolled a blank sheet of paper into the typewriter.

Time clicked by. There were balls of wadded-up paper littering her table, but a thin pile of freshly typed sheets lay at her elbow. This time she would do it, she told herself. And when she was finished, she'd produce, maybe even direct the production herself. She chuckled as she stretched her fingers. Isn't that what she'd told herself whenever she'd begun to write?

Alexander found her that way, hunched over the typewriter, working steadily, with her hair piled on top of her head and her legs drawn up under her. The light was burning on the table and fell across her hands as they moved over the keys. She wore the same blue robe he remembered from the first night he had come to her. She'd pushed the sleeves up to her elbows and it fell carelessly open over her thigh.

Every time he saw her he was freshly amazed at how lovely she was. She exploited her looks when she chose, at other times was negligent of them. It never seemed to matter. Competence. Was that what added so much substance to beauty? Something about her told the onlooker she could do what she set out to do, and do it well.

Her hands appeared delicate, yet she was not. Her shoulders appeared fragile, yet she was strong. Her face was young, vulnerable and so sensitive. Though she might have been all those things, she had a strength and a sense of purpose that made her capable of dealing with whatever life handed her.

Is that why he loved her? For her capabilities? Weary, Alexander passed a hand over his face. He'd only begun to realize this fully, only begun to try to analyze and understand. Attraction had become so much more than an appreciation of beauty. Desire had dipped far beyond the physical.

He'd told her once he'd needed her. It had been true, before that moment and now past it. But he hadn't told her, or fully understood himself, the scope of the need.

When he'd thought he might have lost her, his heart seemed to have stopped beating. He seemed to have stopped seeing, stopped hearing, stopped feeling. Is that what it meant to love?

He wished he could be sure. He'd never allowed himself to love beyond his family and his country. With Eve he hadn't allowed, but had fallen victim to. Perhaps that was love. To be vulnerable, to be dependent, to be needful. Such a tremendous risk, a risk his practicality told him he couldn't afford. Not now, perhaps not ever. Yet it was done.

If he could have one wish at that moment, it would be to take her away somewhere where they could be ordinary people in ordinary times. Maybe tonight, for a few hours, they could pretend it was true.

He watched her straighten, then press her splayed hand against the small of her back.

"You promised you wouldn't overwork yourself."

Her hand stayed where it was, but her head shot around. He saw and recognized the relief, then the pleasure came into her eyes. "This is what we term the pot calling the kettle black." Her gaze swept over him with a greediness that had his fatigue vanishing. "You look tired, Alex. I thought you'd be in bed."

"Meetings." He stepped into the room. "I'm sorry I couldn't be with you this evening."

"I missed you." Their hands met and held. "And I wasn't going to say it, but I worried."

"There was no need." His other hand came up to cover hers. "I've been in the palace since five."

"I wanted to ask, but..." She smiled a little and shook her head. "I guess I didn't feel as if I should."

"Either Bennett or Gabriella could have told you."

"You're here now. Have you eaten?"

"We had something in my father's office." He couldn't have told her what. He couldn't remember any taste, just the reports. "I'm told your sister is here."

"She got in late this morning." Uncurling herself, Eve rose to go to a small rococo cabinet. There she unearthed brandy and two snifters. "She could use some reassurance, which I hope Brie is giving her. She worried herself into a frazzle before she got here."

"Perhaps with her help you could be convinced to go back to America."

Eve handed him a glass, then tapped hers to it. "Not a chance."

"We could reschedule your performances, wait a few months, a year."

Eve sipped with one brow lifted. "Have you spoken to Chris already?"

"No, why?"

"Nothing." She smiled, then walked over to the stereo unit. With a few flicks she had music whispering into the room. When you intended to seduce a prince, she decided, you should pull out all the stops. "I'm not leaving, Alex, so it's a waste of time for us to argue about it." She touched her tongue to the rim of her glass. "I hate to waste time."

"You're a stubborn woman." Just looking at her, just hearing her voice made his pulse race. "Perhaps if I didn't want you with me so badly I could pressure you into leaving."

"No. No, you couldn't. But you don't know how much I've wanted you to say you want me with you." She came to him, so that they stood in front of her desk with the light burning beside them.

"Haven't I told you?"

"No." She took his hand again. "You don't tell me a great deal with words."

"I'm sorry." He brought her hand to his lips.

"I don't want you to be sorry." She set down her snifter. "I don't want you to be anything but what you are."

"Strange." He kept her hand close to his cheek. "There have been so many times recently when I've wished to be anything but what I am."

"Don't." Her strength was what he needed at that moment. Somehow she knew it. "No regrets. There should never be any regrets from either of us for being what we are. Instead let's enjoy." Her thumb ran light and caressing under his jawline. "Just enjoy."

"Eve." He didn't know what he could say to her, what should be said, what was best kept inside for a while longer. Her hand still in his, he started to set down his glass. "I nearly spoiled your papers." He put the glass down beside them. "You work too hard."

"There's that pot and kettle again."

He laughed. It was always easy to laugh when he was with her. "What is this? Another play?"

"It's nothing." She started to gather the papers up, but he put his finger down on them. "I don't know this one. What is this title, *Marking Time*? This isn't one of the alternates."

"No." Embarrassed, she tried to draw his attention away. "It's nothing."

"You're already thinking of producing something else?" He thought about her leaving, going on with her life, her career. With an effort he tried to show interest rather than regret. "What sort of play is it?"

"It's going to be—it's a family drama of sorts. Why don't we—"

"There's so little of it here." With his thumb he flipped through and estimated no more than twelve pages. Then it clicked, the way she'd been hunched over her typewriter, the matted balls of paper. With a quiet smile he looked back at her. "You're writing it."

Caught, she moved her shoulders and tried to draw away. "It's just a hobby."

"You're blushing."

"Of course I'm not. That's ridiculous." She picked up her brandy again and struggled to sound careless. "It's just something I do in my spare time." She swirled the brandy, then drank, and he thought how much he regretted never seeing her on stage.

"*Chérie*, in the past few weeks, I've seen firsthand how little spare time you have." He tucked her hair behind her ear. "You never told me you wanted to write."

"When you're only mediocre you don't broadcast it."

"Mediocre. I'd have to judge that myself." He reached for the pages again, but she was quicker.

"It's very rough. I haven't done any polishing."

"I can respect an artist's temperament about her work not being seen until it's finished." But he intended to see it, and soon. "Is it your first?"

"No." She slipped the papers into a drawer and closed it. "I'd finished one and done part of another."

"Then I'll see the one that's finished."

"It's gone." Again she struggled to keep her voice neutral. "It was in the office."

"Your work was lost." He took a step to her, then framed her face in his hands. "I'm sorry, so sorry, Eve. I would think that whatever one writes is a part of one. Alive. To lose it would be devastating."

She hadn't expected him to understand. Writing, as any art, was emotion as much as skill or technique. Her heart, always open to him, absorbed. "It wasn't a very interesting play," she murmured. "More of a learning tool, really. I just hope I learned enough to make this one better."

"I've wanted to ask you something."

"What?"

"You once wanted to be an actress. Why aren't you acting?"

"Because an actor has to do what he's told. A producer calls the shots."

He had to smile. "As simple as that."

"Added to the fact that I'm a better producer than I ever was an actor."

"And the writing?"

"Sort of a dare to myself." How easy it was to tell him now that she had begun. There was no need for secrets or embarrassment. Not with him. "If I claim to know so much about the theater, what pleases the audience, how to stage and produce a play, why couldn't I write one? A successful one," she added before she drained the brandy. "The first attempt was so miserable I decided I could only get better."

"You enjoy challenging yourself. The theater, fencing, your martial arts."

"I learned, later than most, that challenging yourself means you're alive, not just existing." With a shake of her head she set down her empty glass. "And you're spoiling things."

"I?"

"Yes. You've got me philosophizing, when I was set to seduce you."

"I beg your pardon." His lips curved as he leaned back on the table.

"I suppose you've been seduced before." Eve walked to the door, clicked the lock, then turned back.

"Countless times."

"Really." Her brow lifted as she leaned back against the door. "By whom?"

His smile only widened. "*Mademoiselle*, I was raised a gentleman."

"It doesn't matter," she decided with a wave of her hand. "As long as it wasn't that British blonde you danced with instead of me."

He remained discreet.

"Hmmm. Let's see. I've plied you with brandy. I've added the music. Now I think . . ." A gleam came into her eyes. "Yes, I believe I have just the thing. If you'd excuse me for just a moment."

"Of course."

She swept by him into the adjoining bedroom. Without a qualm, Alexander drew open her drawer and began to read her play. It caught him immediately, the dialogue between a woman no longer young and her reflection in her dressing room table mirror.

"Your Highness."

He slipped the drawer closed before he turned. He wanted to tell her he thought it was wonderful. Even with feelings prejudicing him he knew there was something special in her words. But when he saw her he could say nothing at all.

She wore a teddy skimmed with lace and a long, open robe, both the color of lake water. Her hair was down now, freshly brushed so that it pooled over her shoulders. Behind her light flickered, shifting and swaying. Her eyes were dark. He wondered how it was he could see his own desire reflected in them. Then, as she had the first time, she held out a hand.

He walked to her and his head began to swim from the scent of candle wax and women's secrets. Saying nothing, she drew him into the bedroom.

"I've waited all day to be with you." Standing close, she began to unbutton his shirt slowly. "To touch you." She ran a hand down his flesh before she pushed the shirt over his shoulders. "To be touched by you."

"When I'm away from you, I think of you when I should be thinking of other things." He slipped the robe from her and let it drift to the floor. "When I'm with you, I can think of nothing but you."

The words thrilled her. He said such things so rarely. "Then think of me."

The room was alight with a dozen candles. The bed was already turned down and waiting. Through the doorway came the quiet music, Debussy now, and nothing else. Wordlessly she drew him with her to the bed and began to love him as every man dreams of being loved.

Her first kiss was tender, reassuring, giving, while her hands stroked easily over him. She brushed her lips over his face, his throat, lingering long enough to arouse, not long enough to satisfy. The lace, the silk, the flesh that was her rubbed and shifted over his body until the flame burned hot inside him.

She undressed him, murmuring and brushing away the hands that sought to help her. Her tongue toyed with the back of his knee, drawing a groan from him. Her eyes half-closed, she looked at the body she brought such delight to. He looked gold in the candlelight. Gold and gleaming. She set out to destroy all semblance of control.

He thought his heart would burst through his chest. No woman had ever aroused him so outrageously. Whenever he reached for her, she evaded, then weakened him with a nip of her teeth or a featherlight caress. Agonizing. Magnificent. The breath backed up in his lungs or he might have begged for her to stop. To go on.

Helpless. She was the first ever to have made him helpless. It was a feeling that skittered through his stomach, rippled through his muscles, smoked through his brain. His skin grew damp, hot, sensitized. Wherever she touched brought a myriad of thrills. A moan wrenched out of him and he heard her low, answering laugh.

How incredible to learn that making a man shudder could be so exciting. How satisfying to discover a power that brought only pleasures. Her mind buzzed with the sense of it until she heard nothing else.

Here he belonged to her. If only here. There was no country, no duty, no traditions.

On the edge of reason, he pulled himself up. Hooking an arm around her waist, he dragged her to him, under him. Ranged above her, breath heaving, he stared down. Her chin was lifted. The dare was in her eyes.

"You're my insanity," he murmured, and crushed his mouth to hers.

They were sucked into the whirlwind, each not fighting to be free, but for more velocity. Once they had fenced and struck power against power. Now it was the same.

They rolled over the bed, mouth to mouth, body to body. He stripped her, but not with the care she'd come to expect. His fingers shook as he pulled the brief barrier from between them. They shook, then pressed and gripped, leaving tiny aches behind.

She moaned not from pain, but from the knowledge that his control had snapped. She'd wanted it, dreamed of what she would find behind that firmly locked door. It was on her now, like a beast breaking chains. Violent, desperate, with a primitive kind of relish. He drove her beyond the reasonable into a desire so dark, so thick, she was blind from it.

Shuddering, she crested, and while she was still breathless he pushed her up and over the peak again.

"Alexander." She thought she'd shouted his name, but it was only a gasp. "I want you." Her hands traveled down, grasping, and found him. "I want you inside me."

He knew what madness was, true madness, the moment he felt her close around him. Her hips arched, setting the rhythm. He wanted to watch her face, to know when she had reached as high as it was possible to reach. But his vision was clouded.

The power took them both. When it did, he called out in French. It was the language of his heart.

Chapter Eleven

It was the first time she'd awoken in his arms. The predawn light was smoky gray with a mist that would clear as soon as the sun rose. The sound of the sea was just a whisper through the windows. Candles had gutted themselves out long since, but their scent still hung lightly in the room. He brushed a kiss at her temple and she awoke.

"Alexander." She murmured his name and cuddled closer.

"Go back to sleep. It's early."

She felt him shift away. "You're going."

"Yes, I must."

She wrapped her arms around him and held on to the warmth. "Why? It's early."

He gave a low chuckle, finding her slurred words and sleepy movements endearing. After lifting the arm that held him down, he kissed her hand. "I have early appointments."

"Not this early." She struggled to wake fully. Opening her eyes, she looked at him. His hair was mussed, from the pillow, from her hands, from a night of loving. But in the indistinct light his eyes were alert. "Couldn't you stay an hour more with me?"

He wanted to, wanted to tell her he would spend all the hours of that day and the next with her. But he couldn't. "It wouldn't be wise."

"Wise." She understood, and some of the pleasure faded from her sleep-drugged eyes. "You don't want to be in my room when the servants wake up."

"It's best."

"For whom?"

His brow lifted, part amusement, part arrogance. It was rare for anyone to question him or his motives. "What's between us is between us. I wouldn't care to have you gossiped about or to see your name splashed in the papers."

"As it was with Bennett." There was a touch of anger in her voice as she pushed herself up, leaned back against the headboard and crossed her arms. "I prefer to worry about my reputation myself."

"And you're free to do so." He ran a finger over her bare shoulder. "But I shall worry about it, as well."

"About mine or yours?"

He wasn't a patient man by nature. It was something he'd had to work on step by frustrating step over the years. Now he put as much as he could into practice. "Eve, there's already talk since that picture of the two of us was in the paper."

"I'm glad." She tossed back her hair and watched him steadily. There was hurt. She wasn't sure where it had come from or why it was so acute, but it was there. Hurt could so easily lead to being unreasonable. "I'm not ashamed of being your lover."

"Is that what you think? That I'm ashamed?"

"You come to me late and leave early, before the sun's up, as if you were ashamed of where you spent the night and with whom."

His hand went to her throat, holding there firmly enough for her to feel the strength and the fury behind it. She kept her eyes level, though emotion burned hot and dark in his. "Don't ever say that. How can you even think it?"

"What do I have to make me think differently?"

His fingers tightened on her throat, making her eyes widen in shock before his mouth came down, hard and furious, on hers. She struggled, wanting words, whatever words he would give her, but his hands were quick and desperate. Ruthless, he took them over her, exploiting every weakness he had discovered in more gentle ways.

Her body was a mass of throbbing, pulsing nerves. Any and all coherent thought had fled, to be replaced by sensation after rioting sensation. Her arms locked tight around him, she accepted what he would give. Her body answered his with the same fire and fury.

The edge of temper met the edge of passion. They scraped, grated, then with a merger that was anything but placid, became one.

He lay looking up at the ceiling. She was curled beside him, but they no longer touched. The sun was burning off the mist.

"I don't want to hurt you."

She let out a shaky breath, but her voice was strong and clear when she spoke. "I'm not easily hurt, Alexander."

"Aren't you?" He wanted to reach out, to take her hand in his, but wasn't sure she would accept it. "We need to find a time, a place to talk. It isn't now."

"No, it isn't now."

When he got out of bed, she stayed where she was. She heard him dress, and waited for the sound of the door opening and closing again. Instead she felt a hand light on her shoulder.

"I feel many things for you, but not shame. Will you wait for me at the theater? I'll find a way to be there by six."

She didn't look at him, knowing that if she did she'd beg him to stay, and perhaps beg for a great deal more than he could give. "Yes, I'll wait."

"Sleep awhile longer."

She said nothing. The door opened and closed.

Eve squeezed her eyes tight, fighting a sense of despair and loss. He'd given her passion, but no answers. Once she'd promised herself his passion would be enough. It was a hard blow to learn now that it couldn't be. She wanted his heart, without the restrictions he placed on it. She wanted to be loved, cherished, accepted. What she wanted was more than she could have, and she couldn't live with less.

Understanding this, Eve rose. It was time to begin her life again. There would be no regrets for the dream that had flickered briefly into life.

Alexander walked into his father's library and acknowledged the men already present. His father sat in a wing chair, just crushing out a cigarette. Reeve, with papers on his lap and spread on the table before him, sat on the sofa with Bennett. Malori, the chief of intelligence, sat on the edge of a chair, lighting his pipe.

The men had met the evening before, and would meet again for however long it took to crush the threat Deboque held over them. They began on familiar ground, starting with the security Reeve had implemented at the palace, at the theater, at The Aid to Handicapped Children Center and at his own home. There was additional information regarding the airport and the docks.

"You've assigned an extra detective to each of us," Bennett put in.

"For as long as it's necessary."

He shifted restlessly against the restraint, but accepted it. "Do you really think they'll go through Eve again? They have to know we'd tap the phones and keep her watched."

Malori puffed on his pipe. "Deboque's greatest flaw, Your Highness, is arrogance. I believe his next move will come through Mademoiselle Hamilton, and soon."

"I repeat what I said last evening," Alexander began. "Eve should be sent back to America."

Malori tapped the bowl of his pipe. "That would not stop Deboque, Your Highness."

"It would ensure her safety."

"Alexander." Reeve watched the prince light a cigarette. "If what the investigation has turned up is fact, we need Eve. If she would go," he continued before Alexander could speak. "I'd put her on a plane myself. Since she insists on staying, the solution is to guard her and wait."

"Wait." Alexander blew out a stream of smoke. "Wait for her to be put in jeopardy again. If, as you believe, someone inside the theater placed the calls, planted the bomb, she's in danger even now from one of her own people."

"Deboque isn't concerned with her," Malori said quietly. "She's only a pawn."

"And pawns are expendable."

"Alexander." Armand spoke for the first time. His voice was as quiet as Malori's but held the unmistakable ring of authority. It was a cool voice, often bordering on the cold, but it was rarely harsh. His arms rested on the chair as he paused and looked over his steepled fingers. "We must deal with this calmly, as calmly as Deboque. You understand that I care for Eve as I care for my own children. Everything that can be done to protect her will be done."

"She is not Cordinian." Alexander struggled, emotion, intellect. "She is a guest in our country. We are responsible for her."

"We don't forget our responsibilities." The authority was there. Mixed with it was a compassion that couldn't be given full sway. "If one of Eve's people is an agent of Deboque's, we will learn the identity. Logically Deboque will not order her harmed, or his agent will no longer have a reason to remain in Cordina."

"And if Deboque is not logical?"

"Such men are always logical. There is no passion in them."

"Mistakes can be made."

"Yes." Armand thought of Seward. The grief remained inside. "Mistakes can be made. We must see we don't make any." His gaze shifted to Reeve. "I leave this to you."

"Everything that can be done on the short term is being done. As to the long term, Malori and I have agreed on an operative who will infiltrate Deboque's organization."

"I agreed with reservations," Malori mumbled.

"No need for them." Reeve's lips curved, then he handed Armand a folder. "Malori and I do agree that the identity of this operative should be known only to the three of us."

"It concerns us all," Bennett interrupted.

"Yes." Reeve nodded. "And the life of this operative depends on secrecy. The fewer people who know who is working for us, the better chance we have of succeeding. It may take months, more likely years. You have to understand we're only planting a seed here. It needs time to grow."

"I wish only to see an end to Deboque in my lifetime." Armand kept the file closed. He would look at it later, then lock it in his personal safe. "I want regular reports on the operative's progress."

"Of course." Reeve gathered the rest of his papers. "If we can capture Deboque's agent and interrogate him, perhaps the rest won't be necessary."

As the group of men rose, Alexander addressed his father. "If you have a few minutes, I need to speak with you."

Understanding his brother's need for privacy, Bennett dropped a hand on his arm. "I'm going to go to the theater this morning. I'll keep an eye on her."

Alexander placed a hand over his brother's. There was no need for gratitude to be spoken. "Don't let her know that's what you're doing. She'll kick you out."

"I'll make a nuisance of myself and she'll tolerate me." Then he walked over and kissed his father's cheek. "We are together in this, Papa."

Armand sat where he was, watching until the door closed at his son's back. None of the reports, the files, the plots that had been discussed, had eased his mind. But the simple words, the simple kiss, had done much more than that.

"Of all my children, Bennett is the only one I cannot predict."

"He'd be flattered to hear it."

"As a boy he found every broken bird, every injured kitten, always believing he could make them well again.

Sometimes he did. At times I worry that he feels too deeply. He's so like your mother." Armand shook his head and rose. "Should I order coffee, Alexander?"

"No, not for me. I have to go to Le Havre. Welcome a ship."

"Such enthusiasm."

"I'll show it when the time comes."

"I don't doubt it. This concerns Eve."

"Yes."

With a nod Armand walked to the window to throw it open. Maybe the breeze from the sea would air out some of the tension still in the room. "Alex, I have eyes. I think I understand what you're feeling."

"Perhaps you do. But I've just begun to understand what I'm feeling myself."

"When I was a young man, younger than you, I found myself ruling a country. I had been prepared for it, of course, from the moment of birth. But no one, especially me, had expected it to come so soon. Your grandfather became ill and died in less than three days. It was a difficult time. I was twenty-four. Many members of the council worried about my age and my temperament." He turned then, smiling a little. "I wasn't always as discreet as you have been."

"Bennett was bound to inherit something from your side."

For the first time in days Armand laughed. "I was not quite that indiscreet. In any case, I'd ruled less than a year, when I took an official trip to England. I saw Elizabeth, and all the stray pieces of my life came together. To love like that, Alex, is painful, and more beautiful than anything you can see or touch."

"I know."

Armand turned fully. His breath came out on a long sigh. "I thought perhaps you did. Have you considered what you would be asking of her?"

"Again and again. And again and again I've told myself I can't do it. She'll make all the sacrifices, all the adjustments. I don't even know if I can make her understand just how much her life would change if she accepted me."

"Does she love you?"

"Yes." Then he paused and pressed his fingers to his eyes. "God, I hope she does. It's difficult for me to be certain of her feelings when I've been fighting my own for so long."

This, too, he understood. When he had fallen in love, he had had no father to speak to. "Do you want my approval or my advice?"

Alexander dropped his hand. "Both."

"Your choice pleases me." Armand smiled and walked toward his son. "She will make a princess Cordina can be proud of."

"Thank you." They clasped hands. "But I think being a princess is something that won't please Eve nearly as much as Cordina."

"Americans." Now Armand grinned. "Like your *beau-frère*, she would prefer to avoid such things as titles and positions of state."

"But unlike Reeve, she'd have no choice."

"If she loves you, the crown she'll wear won't be so heavy. Nor will yours, when your day comes."

"If." Alexander let the word hang. "I appreciate your approval, Father. Now your advice."

"There are few people you can open your heart to, open it fully. When you find a woman to share your life, hold nothing back from her. A woman's shoulders are strong. Use them."

"I want to protect her."

"Of course. Doing one doesn't mean not doing the other. I have something for you." He left the library through the connecting door to his office. Moments later he was back with a small black velvet box. He held it tightly in his hand as he went to his son.

"I wondered what I would feel when I gave this to you." He stared down at the box in his hand. "There's regret that it's mine to give again, pride that I have a son to give it to." His emotions, always so well controlled, swirled to the surface and were battled down. "There's pleasure that my son is a man I can respect, not only a boy I love."

He passed it over, hesitating a moment before his fingers broke contact with the box. "Time passes," he murmured. "This is the ring I gave your mother on the night I asked her to marry me. It would please me, when you ask Eve, if you would give her this."

"There's nothing I would be prouder to give her." He couldn't open the box, but his hand gripped it as tightly as his father's had. "Thank you, Papa."

Armand looked at his son, as tall as he. He remembered the boy and all the years in between. He smiled and embraced the man. "Bring her to me when she wears it."

Eve watched two stagehands, armed with spray cans, painting pipe. She stifled a yawn and made a notation. She was definitely going to have to invest in some new equipment once they were back in the States, which was in less than five weeks. In two days the first production would open; four weeks later the last production would close. They'd take a couple of days to break down the last set, then that would be that.

The company was already booked on a road tour through the fall. She was negotiating a three-week run in L.A. for January. And if she didn't miss her guess, her desk would be piled with offers and inquiries after her return from Cordina.

Her return.

Eve walked to the stage manager's desk at stage right and tried to concentrate on the rehearsal. The actors were in full costume and makeup. She couldn't see a flaw. The big red urn she'd commissioned Pete to buy stood out like the beacon she'd imagined. The upholstery on the sofa was faded. The doilies were bright and stiffly starched.

It was perfect. She had organized it, and it was perfect. She wished she could find the pleasure in it that she'd always felt before.

"It looks great."

The whisper at her ear had her jolting. "Ben." She pressed her clipboard against her heart. "What are you doing here? This is supposed to be a closed rehearsal."

"Of course that didn't include me. I explained that to the doorman. Tell me, do you call him 'Pops' like in the American movies?"

"I wouldn't dare." She glanced behind him and saw his guards hovering at a safe and discreet distance. "Shouldn't you be out doing something official?"

"Don't lecture. I've been slaving away for weeks. I stole a couple of hours." The two precious hours he would have spent with his horses. "I just thought I'd stop by and see how things were going."

"If you're looking for Doreen," Eve began dryly, "she's upstairs in Rehearsal Hall B. We do have three other plays to deal with, you know."

"Okay, I can take a hint. I won't distract Doreen while she's rehearsing." The truth was, he hadn't given her a thought. He scanned the stage as the play unfolded. "Most of your people have been with you quite a while, I suppose."

"Some have, some haven't. Look, let's move down to the audience. I haven't had a chance to watch from that angle today."

Bennett went with her, settling in the center aisle, mid-theater. The guards moved in three rows behind. Eve didn't notice there were two more. They had been assigned to her.

"It looks good," she murmured. "I've sat all the way up in the back balcony and it still looks good. The acoustics in this place are simply incredible."

"I guess you get to know your people pretty well," Bennett ventured. "Socially, I mean, not just on a professional level."

"When you take a play on tour you usually do. But, then, actors and theater people are just like everyone else." She smiled as she looked at him. "Some are more sociable than others. Thinking of joining up?"

"Can I get an audition?"

"You might do better applying for a job as a stagehand. They have more opportunity to flirt with the ladies."

"I'll keep that in mind. Just how many people work for you?"

"It varies with the production."

"How about now?"

Brows drawn together, she turned to him again. "Why?"

"Just curious."

"All of a sudden?" she countered. "You're asking a lot of questions you never bothered to ask before."

"Maybe I just thought of them. Ever hear of passing the time?"

"Ben, I know you, and since Reeve asked me some very similar questions yesterday, I have to figure there's a purpose to them. What do my people have to do with the investigation?"

He stretched out his legs, insolently resting them on the seat back in front of him. "Hard for me to say, since I'm not investigating. Eve, I don't believe I've been introduced to the lady onstage in her slip."

"Bennett, don't play games with me. I thought we were friends."

"You know we are."

"Then level with me."

He hesitated only a moment. Because he was her friend, because he respected her, he'd already made up his mind. "Eve, don't you think we should consider all the possibilities?"

"I don't know. You tell me."

"The second call was made from inside the complex." He watched her eyes widen. "I didn't think they had told you. I thought they should."

"You mean here, from the theater?"

"They can't pin it down that specifically. They just know it wasn't made from outside the building. There were guards on every door, every entrance. There was no sign of any break-in. The bomb had to be planted by someone inside. Someone who belongs inside the complex."

"And you're narrowing in on my people." Her protective instinct came first. "Damn it, Ben, there are three other theaters in this complex. How many other actors, technicians, maintenance people?"

"I know, I know." He placed a hand over hers to cut her off. "The point is, it's very likely the person was someone who wouldn't be questioned for being in this theater, backstage, even in your office. Who'd question one of your own, Eve? It's unlikely even you would."

"And why would one of my people threaten your family?"

"I'm told Deboque pays very well."

"I don't believe it, Ben." She turned back to stare at the stage. Her actors, her troupe. Her family. "If I did, I'd scrub this production right now and send everyone home. These people are actors, technicians, seamstresses, for heaven's sake. They're not assassins."

"I'm not saying it has to be—I'm just saying it could be. I only want you to think about it, Eve." His hand pressed down on hers. "And watch yourself. I love you."

All the anger drained. "Ben, if I thought I'd been responsible for bringing someone here who would—"

"Wait, don't even finish. Whatever the answer is, you aren't responsible. Deboque is."

Deboque. It was always Deboque. "I've never even seen him. I don't know what he looks like, and he's pushing into every part of my life. He has to be stopped."

"He will be." Bennett's voice was mild, but she did know him well. The thread of violence ran through it. "Reeve's already started something. It's going to take time, more time than any of us would like, but he's going to be stopped. I just hope I can have a hand in it."

"Keep your hands in your pockets. I don't want anything to happen to you, either."

The touch of violence was gone as he grinned at her. "You don't have to worry about me. I'm more interested in women and horses than I am in glory."

"Just keep it that way." She rose, dragging her hair back with her hand as she did so. "I should go up and check on the other rehearsal."

"You're working too hard, Eve. It's starting to show."

"Gallant. Always gallant."

"You've got to stop worrying about Alex."

"How?"

"All right, so you don't have to stop worrying about him. Try to trust the fates a bit." He rose with her, then reached out to toy with her hair. "He's destined to rule Cordina. I'm not, thank God. Nothing's going to happen to him."

"I always believe that when I see him. I have a harder time when I can't." She kissed him, then decided it wasn't enough and hugged him, too. "I'll see you tonight."

"Play some gin rummy?"

"You already owe me fifty-three dollars from the last time."

"Who's counting?"

"I am." She managed to smile.

He watched her walk down the aisle and back behind the stage. The two guards trailed after her.

Gabriella and Chris came by and tried to convince her to take the afternoon with them at a seaside café. Her assistant brought her coffee and sugar cookies and clucked her tongue. One of the actors offered his dressing room for a

ap and one of the staff from makeup suggested a cream to
elp with the shadows under her eyes.

Eve was steaming by the time rehearsals were wrapped for
he day.

"If one more person, just one more, tells me I should get
ome rest, I'm punching them right in the mouth," Eve
nuttered to herself as she strode down the backstage corri-
lor.

"You won't hear it from me."

Her heels skidded a bit as she stopped. Pete was crouched
over one of his cases, locking up props. "I thought just
about everyone had cleared out."

"Just about have." Keys jingled at his waist as he stood.
'I've got a couple of more things to store. Couldn't find a
oox big enough for that vase or whatever it is."

"Leave it on the set. It's too ugly for anyone to steal."

"You said you didn't want class."

"And you delivered." She rubbed at the tension gnawing
at the back of her neck. "It's perfect—really, Pete. So are
he doilies. I know you're conscientious, but the theater's
going to be locked up tight. With security the way it is
around here, I don't think you have to worry about anyone
making off with the props. Why don't you go get some din-
1er?"

"Thinking about it." Still he hesitated, toying with his
keys.

"Is there a problem?"

"Nope. Got something to say."

Amused, Eve nodded. "Go ahead, then."

"You got my dander up the other day when you ordered
me out of here. Yanked on me, too, and threatened to fire
me."

"I didn't think you were pleased."

"Guess I'd have moved a lot faster if I'd known what was
going on." He scratched his chin and looked at his shoes.
'Talbot told us how you were running around the place,
making sure everybody got out, when you knew there was

a bomb. Seems pretty heroic to me. Stupid," he added looking back at her. "But heroic."

"It wasn't stupid or heroic. It was necessary. But thanks for the thought."

"Like to buy you a drink."

For a moment she was speechless. It was the closest Pete had come to a sociable concession in all the time she'd known him. "I'd like that, too. I have someone meeting me here tonight. How about tomorrow, right after rehearsals?"

"Sounds all right." Pete scratched his chin, shifted his belt, then started down the hall. "You're okay, Ms. Hamilton."

"You, too," she murmured, and felt better than she'd felt all day.

She started down the opposite way, bypassing her old office for her temporary one. Six-fifteen, she thought with a look at her watch. Alexander was late. She'd waited throughout the day, edgy and short of temper, for six o'clock. She'd just have to wait a little longer.

Why did he want to talk to her? To break things off as cleanly as possible. He had to know how deeply in love with him she was. He didn't want to hurt her. Hadn't he said so? He'd want to break things off now, before things became even more difficult for her.

He still wanted her. She had no doubt about that. But there was his sense of honor. He could only offer her a few hours in the night in secret. His sense of right, of fairness, wouldn't allow him to continue for long. Wasn't that one of the reasons she loved him?

No regrets, Eve reminded herself. She'd known things couldn't last and had accepted that from the outset. Princes and palaces—they had no place in her life.

With a sigh she opened the small book she'd put in her briefcase that morning. Inside was the flower she'd pressed, the one Alexander had tucked behind her ear. Two weeks ago? A lifetime ago. She closed the book, telling herself not all women had even that much to comfort them.

You're okay, Ms. Hamilton. Well, that was exactly right. She was okay, and she was going to go on being okay. Life was meant to be faced for what it was.

She would wait, but she wouldn't brood. Going behind her desk, Eve took out one of the new files she'd started to compile.

The theater was quiet. Then she heard the bang.

Chapter Twelve

Eve was halfway out of her seat by the time she heard the footsteps race past her door. Her only thought was to lecture whoever among her troupe was still in the theater, making a commotion, when they were supposed to be at dinner. The moment she reached the doorway she saw the body.

Everything froze. Then she was running down the hall, crouching over the man. There was blood already seeping through his shirt. A tray holding a water pitcher and some glasses had been knocked over. Shards of glass were everywhere. Thinking fast, she tore off the long cardigan she wore and draped it over him.

The phone. She had to get to the phone. Fighting for calm, she ran down the hall again and into her office. Her fingers were damp and trembling when she picked up the receiver and dialed.

"This is Eve Hamilton at the Fine Arts Center, the Grand Theater. A man's been shot. I need an ambulance. The police." Her breath caught as she heard footsteps coming softly toward her door. "Hurry," she whispered. "Please hurry."

She set the receiver on the desk and looked frantically around. There was no way out, no way but the door. The footsteps had stopped, but where? How close? Trembling, she edged around the desk. Whoever it was would kill her, kill her and . . .

Six-twenty. The face of her watch seemed blurred, but she remembered. Alexander. They were waiting for Alexander.

Moisture pearled on her forehead, but she inched closer to the door. She had to warn him somehow. She had to find a way. Even as she reached to pull the door the rest of the way open, it swung slowly toward her.

She saw the gun first. Black, deadly. Then the hand that held it. Biting back a scream, she looked at the face.

The man who had fenced with Alexander. The man who had smiled at her, whose face had seemed vaguely familiar. Now she remembered. He'd been at the theater before.

He wasn't smiling now. His face was grim, set. She looked in his eyes, and knew he was a man who could kill.

"Mademoiselle," he began, and she acted.

She swung, using the back of her fist to connect forcefully with the side of his throat. As the gun clattered out of his hand, she brought her stiffened open hand down on the back of his neck. Panting, she looked down at him, crumpled half in and half out of her office. She wanted to run, just run, but forced herself to think clearly.

Hooking her hands under his arms, she dragged him inside. After a quick fumble through her top desk drawer, she found the key. The room was hardly as long as he was, sprawled on the floor. She stepped over him, shut the door and locked him in.

She shook her head to clear the buzzing that filled it and gave herself a moment, leaning back against the wall and catching her breath. The wounded man a few steps away groaned, and she was beside him instantly.

"Help's coming," she murmured. "You're going to be all right."

"Jermaine..."

"Yes, yes, I know. It's taken care of. You mustn't try to talk." Pressure, she thought. She had to stop the bleeding. She dragged a hand through her hair and tried to think. Towels. "Try not to move," she told him. "I'm going to get something to stop the bleeding."

"Was waiting—was hiding."

"He's locked up," she assured him. "Don't talk anymore. I won't be gone long."

She rose, intending to run to the nearest bathroom for towels, when she heard a noise behind her. She spun around, but the hall was empty. Moistening her dry lips, she stared at her office door. Was he conscious again already? It hit her then, coldly, that she hadn't taken the gun. It was locked in with him. If he woke up and found it . . .

Then she heard voices out front and ran toward them.

The stage was dark. She hit the main switch, flooding the stage with light. Her chest heaved with a sob at the sound of Alexander's voice. As he climbed the steps to the stage she was racing across it. His apology for being later than he'd promised never materialized. He had her by the arms, holding firmly.

"What is it?"

"The man, Deboque's agent—he's locked in my office. He shot a man, one of your guards, I think. I've already called an ambulance and the police."

"Did he hurt you?" Even as he took the first quick look, his hands moved to her shoulder. "There's blood."

"Not mine, the guard's. Alex, he needs attention. And in my office—"

"It's all right." His arm circled her as he turned to his own bodyguards. "See to it. I'll stay here with her."

"He has a gun," she began.

"So do they. Sit." He lowered her to the sofa she had insisted be faded. "Tell me." He took his gaze from hers only long enough to watch his guards go backstage.

"Everyone went home—I thought everyone went home. Of course I know there's been a guard on me. I heard a bang, then footsteps. There was the body in the hall. I went back to the phone, then I heard someone again. Alex, it was the man you fenced with, that Jermaine."

"Jermaine was shot?"

"No, no!" Dragging her hands through her hair, she tried to be clear. "He was the one. He had a gun. I knocked him out, then—"

"You knocked out Jermaine?"

"I'm trying to tell you," she snapped. "He must have shot the other man, and he was coming back."

"Eve." He shook her gently. "Jermaine is the head of my personal security. I assigned him to you to protect you."

"But he..." She trailed off, struggling to clear her mind. "Then who...?"

"I'm sorry to interrupt." Russ stepped out of the shadows at stage left. In his hand was a revolver, lengthened by a slim silencer.

"Oh, my God." Before the words were out, Alexander was up, placing Eve behind him.

"I have to thank you for sending your guards away, even so briefly, Your Highness. I promise to be quick. I am, after all, a professional."

"No." Eve stepped from behind Alexander to grip his arm. "You can't."

"You, I regret." There was a touch of sincerity in his tone as he smiled at Eve. "You know the business, Eve. I want you to know you're the best producer I've ever worked for."

"You won't get away with it." Alex spoke quietly, knowing his guards would be back in a matter of seconds.

"I've been given the opportunity to learn this theater very well. I can disappear in ten seconds. It should be all I need. If I don't make it..." He shrugged. All of them heard the high, distant sound of sirens. "Well, that's business." He leveled the gun at Alexander's heart. "Nothing personal."

They were standing on the set. The red urn with its bunch of bright paper flowers stood out like a joke. The heat of the spotlights warmed them as though the play had already begun. But the gun was real.

She screamed. It was torn out of her. Without a second thought, with no regrets, she stepped in front of Alexander and took the bullet.

* * *

She couldn't die. Alexander sat with his head in his hands as the phrase repeated over and over in his head like a litany. He knew how to pray, but those were the only words that would come to him.

He knew there were others in the waiting room, but they might have been ghosts. Phantoms of his own imagination. His father stood by the window. Bennett sat on the small lounge with Chris's hand in his. Gabriella sat beside Alexander, letting her support come through without words. Reeve was there, then gone, then back again, as he dealt with the police.

If he'd had only a second more, one second, he could have pushed her aside, thrown her aside. Anything to keep the bullet from going into her. She'd jerked against him. As long as he lived, he'd never forget the way her body had jerked in shock and pain before it had gone limp.

And her blood had been on his hands. Literally and figuratively.

"Take some tea, Alex." Gabriella urged the cup on him, but he shook his head. She watched as he lit yet another cigarette. "Don't do this to yourself," she murmured. "Eve is going to need you to be strong, not riddled with guilt."

"I should have protected her. I should have kept her safe." He closed his eyes but could still see that horrifying moment she had swung herself in front of him. Throwing her arms around his body as a shield. "It was me he wanted."

"You or any of us." She put a hand on his knee. "If there's guilt we share it equally. Alex, through the worst days of my life, you were there for me and I wouldn't let you help. Let me help now."

His hand covered hers. It was all he could give.

Reeve came back into the waiting room. He looked at his wife, touched her briefly on the shoulder, then went to Armand, by the window. Armand only nodded, then went back to his silent vigil. He, too, knew how to pray.

Unable to sit any longer, Chris rose and walked to the corridor, then back again. There were tears she hadn't been able to stem drying on her cheeks. She felt Gabriella's arm go around her, and leaned against it.

"We can't lose her."

"No." Gabriella kept her hold tight. "We won't lose her." Gently she drew Chris back toward a chair. "Do you remember when we were in school together, the stories you would tell me about Eve? I had wondered what it was like to have a sister."

"Yes, I remember." Chris took a deep breath and tried to make the effort. "You thought having one would be delightful."

"It seemed I was always surrounded by men and boys." Gabriella smiled and, with Chris's hand in hers, looked around at her family. "You showed me a picture of Eve. She was twelve, thirteen, I think, and beautiful, even as a child. I loved the idea of having someone like that to share things with."

"And I told you how I'd found her in my room with all my makeup lined up on the vanity, experimenting with my best eye shadow. Her eyes looked like garage doors." Chris ran her fingertips under her eyes to dry them. "She thought she looked gorgeous."

Chris sniffed and took the tissue Gabriella handed her. "She hated being sent away to school." Her breath was shaky as she let it out and drew more in. "Dad thought it best, and he was right, really, but she hated it so. We all thought Eve was a lovely girl, a sweet girl, but not too bright. Lord, did she prove us wrong. She just refused to waste her time doing things that held no interest, so she wasted it with magazines or record albums, instead."

"She used to write you those funny letters. You'd read them to me sometimes."

"The ones where she described the girls in the dorm or her history teacher. We should have seen then that she had a knack for the theater. Oh, God, Brie, how much longer?"

"Just a little while," she murmured. "We used to think that she and Bennett... They seemed to suit so well." She looked over at Alexander as he stared down at his own hands. "Isn't it odd that the people we care for should have come together?"

"She loves him so much." Chris, too, looked at Alexander, and her heart rose into her throat. "I wanted her to come back to Houston with me. She couldn't leave him. It was almost as if she knew the time would come when she would protect him." Her voice broke, and she shook her head before going on. "She said it didn't matter how he felt, she only wanted whatever time with him she could have."

Brie sighed. "Alexander closes himself in, so often even from himself. But I don't think there can be any doubt now about his feelings. He blames himself. Not circumstances, not Deboque or fate, but himself totally."

"Eve wouldn't."

"No, she wouldn't."

Understanding, Chris rubbed her hands over her eyes and rose. It wasn't easy to cross the room to him. There was resentment. She couldn't avoid it. There was blame and an anger wedged in her heart that had found no room for escape. The step she took was for Eve. When she sat beside him, he didn't reach out to her, but looked over with eyes that were shadowed and red from the scrubbing of his own hands.

"You must hate me." He said it in a voice that was both quiet and dull. "It is small comfort to know that you can't hate me as much as I hate myself."

She wanted to take his hand for Eve's sake, but couldn't. "That doesn't do Eve any good. She needs us to pull together now."

"I could have found a way to make her leave, to make her go."

"Do you think so?" It made her smile just a little. "I can't imagine that. Since she got out of school Eve hasn't allowed anyone to make her do anything."

"I didn't protect her." He covered his face with his hands again, fighting the pressing need to break down. "She matters more than anything in my life and I didn't protect her."

Chris found her hand groping for his, for Eve, yes, but also for herself and for Alexander. "She stepped in front of you." The pain shot into his eyes again. As her own rose to meet it, their fingers linked. "If you have to blame yourself, Alex, blame yourself for being the man she loves. We have to believe she's going to be all right. I need you to believe that with me, or I don't think I can handle anymore."

They sat and waited. Coffee was brought and grew cold. Ashtrays overflowed. The scent of hospital—antiseptic, detergent and nerves—grew familiar. They no longer noticed the guards posted in the corridors.

When Dr. Franco entered the room, they all got to their feet. His surgical cap was soaked with sweat, as was the front of his pale green scrubs. He came forward and, with the compassion natural to him, took Chris's hand.

"The surgeon is still with her. They'll be bringing her to recovery very soon. You have a strong sister, Miss Hamilton. She doesn't choose to give in."

"She's all right?" Chris's hand gripped the doctor's like a vise.

"She came through the surgery better than anyone could have expected. As I explained, Dr. Thorette is the best in his field. The operation was tricky because the bullet was lodged very near her spine."

"She's not..." Alexander felt his father's hand on his arm and made himself say it. "She won't be paralyzed?"

"It's too early for guarantees, Your Highness. But Dr. Thorette feels there is no permanent damage. I agree with him."

"Your judgment has always been excellent," Armand told him. His voice was rough from cigarettes and relief. "I don't have to tell you that Eve will continue to get the very best care available."

"No, Your Highness, you don't. Alexander." He used the first name, taking the privilege of an old family friend, one he had taken rarely in over thirty years. "She is young, healthy, strong. I give you my word that I can see no reason she won't recover fully. Still, there is only so much we can do. The rest is up to her."

"When can we see her?"

"I'll check recovery and let you know. It's unlikely she'll wake until morning. No, there is no need to argue," he continued, holding up his hand. "I don't intend to tell you that you can't sit with her. I believe it will only help her recovery if you're there when she awakes. I'll go to her now."

There was a low light on as he kept his vigil. Franco had had a tray of food sent up, but Alexander had only toyed with it and pushed it aside.

She lay so still.

He'd been told she would, that the sedation had been heavy, but he watched her for a movement, for a flicker.

She lay so quietly.

An i.v. fed into her wrist; the white bandage holding the needle in place stood out in the dark. A line of machines kept up a steady click and beep as they monitored her. From time to time he stared at the fluorescent green lights. But almost always he stared at her.

Sometimes he spoke, holding her hand in his as he talked of walking together on the beach, of taking her to the family retreat in Zurich or sitting in the gardens. Other times he would simply sit, watching her face, waiting.

He thought how much she would dislike the dull hospital gown they had put her in. And he thought of the lace and silk she had worn the last time they had made love. Only one night ago. He pressed her hand against his cheek as his breathing grew jerky and painful. The touch helped soothe.

"Don't let go," he murmured. "Stay with me, Eve. I need you, and the chance to show you how much. Don't let go."

He sat through the hours of the night fully awake. Just as the slats in the window shade let in the first slivers of light, she stirred.

"Eve." He gripped her hand in both of his. The safety bar on the side of the bed was down so that he could lean toward her. "Eve, you're all right. I'm here with you. Please, open your eyes. Can you hear me? Open your eyes, Eve."

She heard him, though his voice sounded hollow and distant. Something was wrong. She felt as though she had been floating, and the dreams... Her eyelids fluttered, came up. She saw only gray, then blinking, began to make out form.

"I'm here with you," Alexander repeated. "You're going to be fine. Can you hear me?"

"Alex?" She saw his face. It was very close, but she couldn't seem to reach up and touch. It was shadowed with beard. It made her smile a little. "You haven't shaved."

Then she went under again.

Though it seemed like hours to him, it was only minutes later when she stirred again. He was sitting on the bed beside her. This time her eyes focused long enough for understanding to come into them.

"You're not hurt?" Her voice was weak and wavery.

"No, no."

"Russ..."

Involuntarily his fingers tightened on hers. "He's been taken care of. You're not to worry."

But she'd turned her head, seen the machine, realized the rest of it. "Not the hospital." At the panic in her voice he brought her hand to his lips.

"Just for a little while, *ma belle*. Just until you're well."

"I don't want to stay here."

"I'll stay with you."

"You won't go?"

"No."

"Alex, you won't lie to me?"

"No." He pressed kisses to her wrist, comforting himself with the feel of her pulse.

"Am I going to die?"

"No." Now he put a hand to her face and bent closer. "No, you're not going to die. Dr. Franco says you're—" he remembered Eve's own phrase "—healthy as a horse."

"I don't think he put it that way."

"That's what he meant."

She smiled, but he saw the quick wince.

"You have pain."

"It feels like—I don't know. My back, under the shoulder."

Where the bullet had been. It had lodged there instead of in his heart. He kissed her cheek and rose. "I'll call the nurse."

"Alex, don't leave."

"Just to call the nurse. I promise." But he found Franco coming down the hall. "She's awake. She's having some pain."

"All of it can't be avoided, Your Highness. Let me examine her, then we can give her something." He signaled to a nurse.

"She's afraid to be here."

"I understand she has a phobia about hospitals. I'm afraid we can't have her moved just yet."

"Then I'll stay with her."

"I can't permit that, Your Highness."

Even without sleep, with fatigue and worry dragging at him, Alexander was royal. "I beg your pardon?"

"I can't permit you to remain twenty-four hours a day. I will, however, permit you to take shifts with Miss Hamilton's sister or anyone else who gives her comfort. Now I must examine my patient."

Alexander watched him walk into Eve's room, then he sank down on a chair outside the door. God, he needed to be alone for just a few minutes, to find some dark, quiet room where he could finally let go of the rage, the pain, the fear.

She'd spoken to him. She'd looked at him. Her fingers had moved in his. He had that now. Leaning back against the wall, he closed his eyes for the first time in more than twenty-four hours.

He opened them again the moment Franco stepped into the hall.

"You can go in, Your Highness. I've explained to Eve about her condition. I've also assured her that she can have someone with her as long as she likes. I'm going to call her sister now. When Miss Hamilton arrives, I insist you go home, eat a decent meal and sleep. If not, I will bar you from her room."

Alexander passed a hand over the back of his neck. "Dr. Franco, if I didn't know that you had Eve's welfare in mind, I'd simply ignore you."

"It wouldn't be the first time I've gone head to head with a member of your family, Your Highness."

"I'm well aware of that, too. Tell me how she is this morning."

"Weak, of course. But her vital signs are good. She feels her legs and can move them."

"Then there's no—"

"No paralysis. She needs, rest, care and support. I hope to have her out of the ICU by tomorrow, but Dr. Thorette will want to examine her first."

"Dr. Franco, I don't have the words to tell you how grateful I am."

"Your Highness, I've always considered it an honor to treat members of the royal family."

Alexander looked back at Eve's door. The ring box made the slightest of weights in his pocket. "You've always been perceptive."

"Thank you, Your Highness. And I have your word that you will leave soon after Miss Hamilton arrives?"

"You have it."

Alexander went back into the room and found Eve awake and staring at the ceiling.

"I thought you'd gone."

"I promised I wouldn't. Chris will be coming. I'll have to leave then for a little while." He sat beside her again, taking her hand. "But I'll be back. You won't be alone."

"I feel like such a fool—like a little girl, afraid of the dark."

"I'm only relieved to learn you're afraid of something."

"Alex, the guard who was shot. Is he—"

"He's still alive. Everything that can be done is being done to keep him that way. I intend to look in on him when I leave you."

"He might have saved my life," she murmured. "And yours. I don't know his name."

"Craden."

She nodded, wanting to remember it. "And Jermaine?"

He hadn't known how good it would feel to smile again. "Recovered, except for his pride."

"There's no reason for him to be ashamed. I didn't earn my black belt by batting my eyes."

"No, *chérie*, it's obvious you didn't. When you're better, you can explain that to Jermaine." He brushed at her hair, just needing to touch. "What kind of flowers shall I bring you? Something from the garden? I've never asked what your favorite is."

Tears welled up in her eyes and began to spill over.

"Don't." He kissed her fingers, one by one. "Don't cry, my love."

"I brought him here." She closed her eyes, but the tears squeezed through. "I brought Russ to Cordina, to you."

"No." He kept his fingers gentle as he stroked her tears away. "Deboque brought him. We can't prove it, but we know it. You have to know it."

"How could he have deceived me so completely? I auditioned him. Alex, I'd seen his work onstage. I'd talked to people who'd worked with him. I don't understand."

"He was a professional. An excellent actor, Eve, who used that to cover his real vocation. He killed for money.

Not for passion, not for a cause, but for money. Even our security check showed nothing. Reeve's working with Interpol right now, hoping to learn more."

"It all happened so fast it doesn't even seem real."

"You aren't to think of it now. It's over."

"Where is he?"

He debated only a moment, then decided she deserved the truth. "He's dead. Jermaine shot him only seconds after..." But he wasn't quite ready to speak of the way her body had jerked and crumpled against his. "He regained consciousness briefly, long enough for Reeve to get some information. We can talk of all of this later, when you're stronger."

"I thought he would kill you." The new medication was taking effect. Her eyes drooped.

"You saw that he didn't. How should I repay you for saving my life?"

Drifting under, she smiled. "I like bluebells. Bluebells are my favorite."

He brought them every day. When she was permitted to leave the hospital in the care of a private nurse, he brought them to her room. As the first week passed, she began to fret about her troupe. When she did, the little ball of fear that had remained lodged inside him loosened. She was getting well.

The press hailed her as a heroine. Bennett brought the articles up and read them to her, rolling his eyes at the praise and calling her a glory hound.

Eve insisted that the first play open, then worried that something would go wrong without her being there to fix it.

She read the reviews, dissecting each word. It thrilled her that the play was well received, relieved her that Russ's understudy had turned in a sterling performance. It depressed her that she hadn't seen for herself.

She submitted to the examinations with less and less grace as they went on.

"Dr. Franco, when is all this poking and prodding and fussing going to stop? I feel fine."

She was lying on her stomach while he changed the dressing on her wound. The sutures had come out the day before and the healing was clean.

"I'm told you're not sleeping well at night."

"It's because I'm bored to death. A walk in the garden becomes an event. I want to go to the theater, Doctor. I've missed the first production altogether. Damn it, I don't want to miss the opening of the second one."

"Mmmm-hmmm. I'm told you've been refusing your medication."

"I don't need it." She pillowed her head on her hands and scowled. "I told you I feel fine."

"I've always considered grumpiness a sign of recovery," he said mildly as he helped her to turn over.

"I'm sorry if I'm not behaving very well." She drew together the bed jacket her father had brought her.

"No, I don't believe you are."

She had to smile. "Maybe not, but with everyone hovering around me. Dr. Franco, you can't imagine what it's like to be scrutinized. If Chris hadn't convinced my father to go back to Houston, I'd have gone crazy. He was wonderful, of course. Everyone has been. The children have been drawing me pictures. Dorian smuggled in a kitten. You're not supposed to know about that."

"I will consider it privileged information."

"Prince Armand has come in every day. He brought me this music box." She reached over to touch the small hammered silver case on her nightstand. "It was his wife's. He gave it to her when Alex was born, and he said she would want me to have it."

"Because each of you gave him his son."

"Dr. Franco, I don't feel like a hero." The tears started up again, as they had so often in the past few days. She hated them, hated being so prone to them. "I feel like a mess. I need to get on with my life, let other people get on with theirs. I have too much time to think lying here."

"Your thoughts trouble you?"

"Some of them. I need to be busy again."

"Why don't we try an experiment?"

"As long as it doesn't involve another needle."

"No. You will sleep this afternoon."

"Doctor—"

"Ah, wait until you hear the bargain before you complain. You will sleep this afternoon," he repeated. "Then this evening, you will get up and put on your most elegant dress. I suggest a high back for a little while yet. You will go to the theater—" He paused as the light came into her eyes. "As an observer only. You will come directly back to the palace after the play. Perhaps we could allow a light supper. Then, like Cinderella, you will be back in bed by midnight."

"Deal." She stuck out her hand. As they sealed the bargain, she promised herself she would be back to work before the week was out.

Both Chris and Gabriella helped her dress. Eve conducted her own experiment and asked herself if the process tired her. It didn't. She felt exhilarated. After studying the result with the white tube dress and beaded jacket, she decided she looked better than she had before the incident. She was rested, her color was up, her eyes were clear. She drew her hair back with silver combs, added a cloud of scent and felt like a woman again.

"You're beautiful." Alexander took both of her hands as he came to lead her downstairs. He was dressed in formal black and carried a small spray of bluebells.

"I wanted you to think so." With a smile she took the flowers and drew in the scent. Whenever she did so in the future, she knew she would think of him. "This is the first time in days you haven't looked at me as though I were un-

der a microscope. No, don't say anything. I feel like a pris-
oner making good her escape.''

"Then you should make it in style."

He drew her hand through his arm and led her downstairs. There was a limo waiting outside, its motor already
purring. Eve shot Alexander a brilliant smile as she stepped
in.

Champagne was chilling. Beethoven was playing softly.

"The perfect getaway car," she murmured as he released
the cork from the bottle.

"I intend for everything to be perfect tonight."

She touched her glass against his, then her lips against his.
"It doesn't get any better than this."

"We'll see." He reached in a small compartment and
drew out a long, slender box. "I wanted to wait until you
were recovered to give you this."

"Alex, I don't need presents."

"I need to give you one." He opened her hand and placed
the box in it. "Don't disappoint me."

How could she refuse him? Eve opened the lid and stared
down at the necklace of diamonds and sapphires. They
seemed to hang on threads of silver and dripped down in
two layers of teardrops. It was something for a princess, a
queen, not an ordinary woman, she thought. Unable to resist, she lifted it up, and the gems glistened in her fingers.
Lights from streetlamps rushed over them and caught fire.

"Oh, Alex, it's wonderful. It takes my breath away."

"You've often had that effect on me. Will you wear it tonight?"

"I—" It almost frightened her, the sheer beauty of it, the
elegance. But he'd asked almost as if he'd expected her to
refuse. "I'd love to. Help me?"

He unclasped the gold filigree collar she wore and replaced it with his gift. Instinctively Eve brought a hand up
to touch the necklace as he draped her neck. It was cool, but
already drawing on the warmth of her flesh.

"I'm probably going to pay more attention to this than the play." She leaned over to kiss him, a kiss he returned with a surprising delicacy. "Thank you, Alexander."

"Thank me only when the evening is finished."

She was nervous when she entered the theater. Then she was stunned when she entered the royal box and the crowd below rose to its feet to cheer her.

She found her hand caught in Alexander's. There was a smile in his eyes as he bent over and kissed it. Though she felt the emotion swirling, she managed to smile in return, and taking his lead, acknowledged the crowd with a curtsy.

Alexander held her chair with great satisfaction. She had yet to realize it, but she had just completed her first official duty.

"It has to be good." She tried not to squirm as she waited for the curtain to rise. "I wish I could slip backstage for just a minute and see—"

"I have the doctor's orders, *chérie.*"

"I know, but— Oh, God, here goes."

She held his hand tightly throughout the first act. Felt her stomach churn time and time again. Mentally she made a list of every small flaw or break in pacing. She thought of half a dozen changes that would improve it.

But there was laughter. Pride in her troupe, in herself, settled firmly as she heard it. The dialogue was sharp, often acerbic and very American, but the theme of a bumpy romance was international.

When it was over, she counted the curtain calls.

"A dozen." She turned, laughing to Alexander. "A dozen of them. It was good. It was really, really good. I want to change the blocking just a bit in the second scene, but—"

"You won't think about blocking tonight." He took her hand and led her out of the box. Three guards stood at attention. She tried not to notice them, to think only of the play.

"I don't know if I can stand to wait until the reviews come in. Alex, couldn't we go backstage for just a minute so that I can—"

"Not this time." With the guards flanking them, he led her down the side steps. There were reporters, and cameras flashed, but security held the media in check. Before Eve had blinked the lights out of her eyes, they were back in the limo.

"It went too quickly." She leaned back, trying to absorb it all. "I wanted it to last and last, yet I was so nervous. It seemed like everyone was looking at us."

"It made you uncomfortable."

"Only a little." That was already past. "I'm going to convince Franco to let me watch from the wings tomorrow."

"You're not tired?"

"No. Honestly." She smiled as she drew in a deep breath. "I feel incredible. I suppose Cinderella felt the same five minutes before midnight."

"You have an hour yet. I'd like you to spend it with me."

"Down to the last minute," she promised.

The palace was quiet when they returned. He led her upstairs, but instead of taking her to her rooms, he turned to his own.

There was a table set for two, with candles flickering in crystal holders. This time the music was violins, as sensuous as it was romantic.

"Now I really do feel like Cinderella."

"I had planned to do this before, on the night—the night I was to meet you at the theater."

She'd walked over to touch the petals of the flowers spread in a low bowl on the table. "You had?" Surprise and nerves mixed together as she turned. Did a man set such a scene to break off an affair? She didn't think so, not even if the man was a prince. "Why?"

"It seems I've given you too little romance, since you are so stunned by it. It's something I intend to make up for." He came to her, gathered her close and kissed her as he had longed to for days. "I thought I might have lost you." His voice roughened with emotion as he took both her hands and buried his face in them. "I've made so many mistakes with you, but that one—"

"Alex, don't. If you wouldn't let me blame myself for bringing Russ here, how can you blame yourself for what he did?"

"And what you did." He moved his hands from hers, to her face. "As long as I live I'll remember that instant you stepped in front of me. I'll relive it, but each time I do, I'll have pushed you aside in time."

There was such suffering in his voice, such bitterness, that the truth came out without a thought to pride. "If he had killed you, do you think I would have wanted to live? You're all that matters. I've loved you since long before I understood what love meant."

His breath came out like a prayer. No more mistakes, he promised himself. He would do this right. She had not only given him life, but a reason to live it.

"Would you sit?" he asked her.

"Please, don't thank me again. I just can't bear it."

"Eve, sit down." Impatience shimmered in his voice. Because she was more comfortable with that, she obliged.

"All right, I'm sitting. But I'm not being fed over here."

"You'll have all the dinner you want after I get through this." Nerves were eating at him. He waited a moment until he had them under some kind of control. When he knelt at her feet, Eve's eyes widened.

"I said I wouldn't kneel for you. This one time it seems appropriate." When he drew a box out of his pocket, her hand closed into a fist.

"Alex, you've already given me a gift tonight." Her voice, usually so rich and smooth, shook.

"This isn't a gift. It's a request, the biggest one I could ask of you. I've wanted to ask you before, but it seemed too much to expect."

Her heart was thudding, but she kept her fingers curled together. "You don't know what to expect unless you ask."

He laughed and, taking her hand, spread her fingers open. "You always show me something new. Eve, I'm going to ask you for more than I could ever give. I can only tell you that if you agree, I'll do everything in my power to make you happy."

He placed the box in her hand and waited.

First she had to draw a breath, a long one. She was not an aristocrat; she was not of royal blood. Equal terms. She remembered her own demand and realized she had the chance to make it all real.

She opened it and saw a ring with the same design of sapphires and diamonds as the necklace she was wearing. Not a gift, she thought, but a request.

"It was my mother's. When I told my father I intended to ask you to marry me, he asked that I give you this. It's more than a ring, Eve. I think you know some of the duties, the expectations that go with it, not just to me, but to the country that would have to be yours, as well. Please, don't say anything yet."

There were nerves in his voice, something she'd never heard before. It made her want to reach out and soothe him, but she stayed still.

"There are so many things I would have to ask you to leave behind. Houston would be only a place to visit. Your troupe—there is the theater here and the opportunity to build a new troupe in Cordina, but the rest would be over. There is your writing—perhaps in some ways that would make up for what you would have to leave behind. Your freedom would be limited in a way you can't imagine. Responsibilities, some of them vital, others incredibly boring. What you do, what you say, will be common knowledge almost before it's done. And as long as Deboque remains alive, there is a very real danger. We've begun something, but it will be a long, long time before Deboque is no longer a threat. These are things you have to know, to consider."

She looked at him, then at the ring still in its bed of velvet. "It seems you're trying to convince me to refuse."

"I only want you to know what I'm asking of you."

"You're a fair and practical man, Alexander." As she took a deep breath, something beyond his shoulder caught her attention and imagination. She didn't smile, not yet. "Let's consider this then in a fair and practical manner." Reaching over, she drew the scales closer. "Let's see, we have the duties and responsibilities of state." There were some glass balls in a jar. She took a handful and placed two on one of the scales. "Then there's the lack of privacy." She added another ball.

"Eve, this is no game."

"Please, I'm trying to think this through. There's the fact that I would no longer live in my own country." Three balls were added. "And the fact that I would very possibly be bored to tears by some of those functions I know Brie has to attend. There's the press, the paperwork—I believe you left that out—and the traditions I'd have to learn." Plus the new ones she'd do her best to begin. "Then there's Deboque."

She looked back at Alexander. "I won't add any pretty colored balls for Deboque. Whether I agree or refuse, he remains who he is. Now, Alex, I have to ask you one question. Why do you want me to take this ring and the responsibilities that go with it? Why are you asking me to marry you?"

"Because I love you."

Now she did smile. The rest of the weights went in the empty scale and brought it down. "That seems to more than even things out, doesn't it?"

He looked at them in a kind of wonder. "I had to say nothing else?"

"That's all you've ever had to say." Throwing her arms around him, she brought him to her for a kiss, a bargain sealed, a life begun. She laughed and pressed her lips to his throat. "Fairy tales," she said, half to herself. "I'd stopped believing in them."

"And I." His lips found hers again. "But no more. Tonight you've given me even that."

"Oh, listen." The clock in the hall outside began to chime. "Put the ring on, Alex, before it strikes twelve."

He slipped it on, then kissed the delicate skin just above the jewels. "Tomorrow we'll tell the world, but tonight this is only for us." He rose then and drew her to her feet. "I haven't fed you, and it's after midnight."

"I could eat in bed. Alex." She rested her cheek against his chest, holding onto the magic. "Franco didn't say I had to get into bed alone."

He laughed as he swept her up. "Cordina is in for many surprises."

"So are you," she murmured.

* * * * *

Don't miss the exciting conclusion of the Cordina trilogy in THE PLAYBOY PRINCE, Language of Love #39, and watch Prince Bennett discover love amidst danger.

COMING NEXT MONTH!

Nathan found lifelong happiness in LOVING JACK—because Jack loved him right back! Now, will Jack find a publisher for her historical romance? Find out next month in BEST LAID PLANS, when Jack's career as a romance writer really takes off—as does a romance between Nathan's partner, Cody, and a lovely structural engineer named Abra.

Both Abra and Cody have definite ideas about construction, architecture and design. Problem is, just about all their ideas clash! But they have an Arizona resort to build together—not to mention an irresistible attraction to each other—and simply must put their differences aside. They soon discover there is no blueprint for a relationship, no carefully drafted plan to follow and there are more surprises and dangers in life and love than on any construction site.

With typical flair, Nora Roberts takes you on the most important journey of all, straight into the hearts and minds of two people falling in love. Don't miss BEST LAID PLANS.

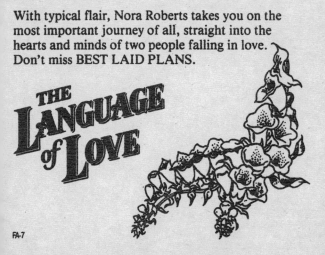

THE
LANGUAGE
of LOVE